Gingerbread Tracks
& Pine Needle Pasta

Gingerbread Tracks & Pine Needle Pasta

A Savory Guide to Yellowstone National Park

MELANIE ARMSTRONG

TAYLOR TRADE PUBLISHING
Lanham • New York • Dallas • Boulder • Toronto • Oxford

Published by Taylor Trade Publishing
An imprint of The Rowman & Littlefield Publishing Group, Inc.
4501 Forbes Boulevard, Suite 200
Lanham, Maryland 20706

Distributed by NATIONAL BOOK NETWORK

Library of Congress Cataloging-in-Publication Data

Armstrong, Melanie, 1977–
    Gingerbread tracks and pine needle pasta : a savory guide to Yellowstone National Park / Melanie Armstrong.
        p. cm.
    Includes bibliographical references and index.
    ISBN 1-58979-190-8 (pbk. : alk. paper)
    1. Cookery. 2. Yellowstone National Park. I. Title.
    TX714.A755 2005
    641.5—dc22   2004024321

♾™ The paper used in this publication meets the minimum requirements of American National Standard for Information Sciences—Permanence of Paper for Printed Library Materials, ANSI/NISO Z39.48–1992.
Manufactured in the United States of America.

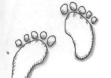

Contents

Preface vii

⇢ Preface ⇠

The valleys at the heads of the great rivers may be regarded as laboratories and kitchens, in which . . . we may see Nature at work as chemist or cook, cunningly compounding an infinite variety of mineral messes, cooking whole mountains; boiling and steaming flinty rocks to smooth paste and mush . . . making the most beautiful mud in the world.   —John Muir[1]

A trip to Yellowstone National Park is a feast for the senses. A day in the park draws our eyes from geysers to wildlife to waterfalls, while our ears record the sound of gushing water or the call of a chickadee hidden in a meadow. As we walk the boardwalks, we plug our noses against the smell of "rotten eggs," later releasing them to inhale deeply the fresh mountain air. At night, gathered around a campfire, we feel the heat of the flame on our fronts, while our backs shiver against the cold of a Yellowstone night. Throughout our visit perhaps we are the least aware of our sense of taste, though we rely on it all day long. Remember the ice cream cone that dripped over your hand while you were waiting for Old Faithful? Or the unforgettable taste of s'mores made from marshmallows cooked over an open fire? Tastes are entwined with our

memories of Yellowstone. In the following pages, taste will become a way to learn and understand the geology, biology, and history of our first national park.

The phenomenon of Yellowstone—with water that shoots out of the ground, wildlife that placidly grazes ten feet from the road, storms that leave behind six inches of snow in July—is a challenge to take in, let alone understand. One of the best ways to comprehend the incomprehensible is to compare it to something familiar. And what could be more familiar to us than food? While walking the boardwalks at Old Faithful, it is not unusual to hear, "Look! That pool is full of lemonade." or "Listen! That sounds like bacon on the griddle." Rangers do it too, comparing the massive eruption of an ancient volcano to the more commonplace event of baking a pie. The natural forces that act on the features in Yellowstone also act on the food in our kitchens. Through such analogies we begin to understand the historical and contemporary events that kneaded, boiled, baked, and blended the Yellowstone landscape.

As you prepare the recipes that follow, your kitchen will become a laboratory for discovering how Yellowstone works and why it looks the way it does. Ultimately, all of Yellowstone, including the geysers, forests, wildlife, and even the establishment of the national park, is the result of geologic activity, so geology is the natural starting point for our olfactory exploration of Yellowstone. Chapters 2 and 3 move on to discovering the animals and plants that live on this high plateau of bubbling mud and periodic explosions of steam and magma. Humans enter the Yellowstone story in chapter 4, which considers the historical importance of food in the region. The book concludes with the important moments of taste we experience when traveling in Yellowstone today.

How Do I Puree My Bear Jam?

When you visit Yellowstone, some of the strange words you hear may make you think you are traveling in a foreign country. It doesn't take too long to catch on: "bear jam" means there's an animal near the road causing traffic to slow; a "fumarole" is a steam vent; and animals in "the rut" aren't stuck in a ditch but looking for mates. Knowing this vocabulary will make your visit to Yellowstone go more smoothly, and knowing a few cooking terms ahead of time will make this cookbook much easier to understand. As you venture further into this cookbook, you may encounter some of the following terms:

A **Dutch oven** is a heavy pot or kettle made of cast iron and with a tight lid. Dutch ovens are used for slow cooking, often over an open fire.

To **boil** is to cook a liquid at the temperature where bubbles rise continuously to the surface. To **simmer** is to cook the liquid just below the boiling temperature, so tiny bubbles rise along the edges of the pan, breaking just beneath the surface.

To **sauté** food is to brown it quickly over high heat using a small amount of fat or grease. **Toasting** also turns food brown, but it is done in a dry skillet or hot oven set to broil.

When this cookbook uses the term **chop**, it means to cut the food into pieces about the same size. To **slice** refers specifically to cutting items into pieces that are narrower in one dimension (in other words, long and narrow instead of square on all sides).

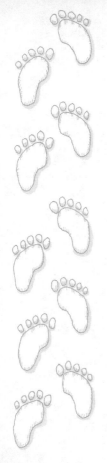

To **puree** is to process food into a smooth paste. **Mashing** food also involves crushing food, but the resulting paste will still be lumpy.

To **marinate** means to soak food in a sauce for a specified length of time. The purpose of marinating is to make food more flavorful, moist, and tender. Always refrigerate food items while they are marinating.

Safety First!

People who come to Yellowstone enter a strange world full of hazards unknown to them in their home environments. Boiling temperatures, wild animals, and fellow travelers threaten human safety everyday. The National Park Service is committed to ensuring that every visitor to Yellowstone leaves with wonderful memories and photographs, not broken bones and blistered burns. Rules and regulations have been established to protect humans from one another (obey speed limits on narrow, winding roads), animals (do not approach wildlife within 25 yards, bears within 100 yards), and geologic hazards (stay on boardwalks and trails in thermal areas).

You should exercise the same sort of care when you are cooking, though the odds of a bison charging you in your kitchen are quite slim. This cookbook is designed for chefs of all ages, but young chefs should always cook with a parent or other adult. Read through each recipe before beginning and then follow directions precisely.

A few other safety tips:

- Never leave cooking food unattended.

- Use potholders when handling hot objects.

- Use a sharp knife for all cutting tasks: the odds of slicing a finger are much higher with a dull knife.

- Keep handles on pots and pans turned inward, away from the reach of curious hands. When possible, use a back burner to keep hot pots out of the reach of children.

- Unplug appliances when not in use. Be careful that appliance cords do not dangle over the edge of the countertop.

- Be cautious in handling food heated in the microwave. Though the container may not feel hot, the liquid inside may be scalding. If children are removing items from the microwave, make sure they can do so without reaching above their heads. This minimizes the risk of hot foods scalding a child's face and arms.

- Watch out for steam, which can cause serious burns. Stand back when removing a pot lid or opening an item heated in the microwave.

- If a grease fire breaks out on top of the stove, cover it quickly with a pan lid or another large pan. You may also use baking soda to smother the fire, but *do not throw water on a grease fire*.

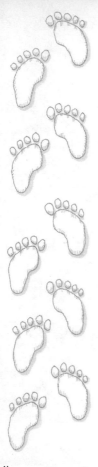

If the fire is in an oven or a microwave, leave the door closed and turn the appliance off. If the door is tightly closed, the fire will smother for lack of oxygen. Do not open the door, which would allow oxygen to feed the flames.

Keep a portable fire extinguisher in your kitchen. Check it frequently and be sure you know how to use it.

NOTE

1. Cited in Paul Schullery, *Old Yellowstone Days* (Boulder: Colorado Associated University Press, 1979).

Chapter One

Volcanoes and Geysers

ellowstone National Park sits atop one of the largest volcanoes in the world. A chamber of magma, three to eight miles below the earth's surface, draws heat from the center of the earth to power the geysers, hot springs, fumaroles, and mud pots we see in Yellowstone. Ultimately, geologic forces not only drive the geysers and hot springs but also determine what kinds of plants and animals can live here, what the weather will be like, and even who will be able to live around the geysers and hot springs. These same natural forces that move rocks and water in Yellowstone also act on the objects of our everyday lives—even the food we eat.

CALDERA-BERRY PIE

As you drive through Yellowstone, you will notice that the center of the park—where all the geysers and hot springs are located—is rather flat. Sure, there are a few hills here and there, but nothing like the jagged peaks of the Tetons to the south or the rows of mountains north of the park in the Absaroka Range. What you are seeing (and driving through) is the Yellowstone caldera, a massive volcanic crater.

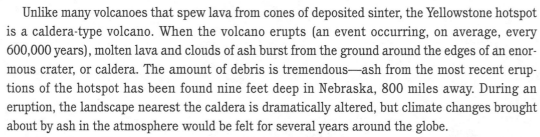

Unlike many volcanoes that spew lava from cones of deposited sinter, the Yellowstone hotspot is a caldera-type volcano. When the volcano erupts (an event occurring, on average, every 600,000 years), molten lava and clouds of ash burst from the ground around the edges of an enormous crater, or caldera. The amount of debris is tremendous—ash from the most recent eruptions of the hotspot has been found nine feet deep in Nebraska, 800 miles away. During an eruption, the landscape nearest the caldera is dramatically altered, but climate changes brought about by ash in the atmosphere would be felt for several years around the globe.

Caldera-Berry Pie simulates an eruption of the Yellowstone hotspot. Prepare the piecrust as directed below, then fill the crust with a gooey red filling of your choice (you can use the cherry filling recipe below, if you wish). Watch the pie as it is baking to see what happens as things heat up.

Piecrust (for one 9-inch pie, including top crust)

⅔ cup plus 1 tablespoon shortening
2 cups flour

⅔ teaspoon salt
5–6 tablespoons cold water

Mix together flour and salt. Work shortening into dry ingredients until crumbs are the size of peas. Add water, one tablespoon at a time, mixing with a fork until evenly moistened and pastry just begins to form a ball. Gather pastry into two balls, one slightly larger than the other.

On a lightly floured surface, roll the larger ball of pastry into a circle less than ¼ inch thick and about 2 inches larger than the size of the pie plate. Gently fold pastry in half, then fourths. Place folded pastry in pie plate, unfold, and shape to the plate by pressing sides and bottom.

Allow excess pastry to hang over the rim of the pie plate.

Pour desired filling into the unbaked crust. The filling should come close to, but not touch, the rim.

Roll remaining pastry into a circle. Fold into fourths and unfold on top of filling. Trim overhanging edges of top and bottom crust at rim of pie plate, turning edges up and pressing together lightly. Place pie plate on a large cookie sheet, *larger than the diameter of the pie plate*. Place cookie sheet and pie plate into preheated oven.

Bake at 425 degrees for 35–45 minutes.

Berry Pie Filling

6 cups fresh berries or cherries	½ cup flour
or 6 cups frozen fruit, thawed and drained	2 tablespoons water or lemon juice
or 3 16-ounce cans of fruit, drained	1 tablespoon margarine or butter
1 cup sugar	

Combine flour and sugar in mixing bowl. Add fruit, stir. Pour mixture into unbaked bottom crust. Cut butter into small chunks, then sprinkle over surface of pie. Cover with top crust.

What Happens?

Watch your pie as it bakes, preferably through a glass window on your oven door or periodically by cracking the oven open. As the filling heats, its molecules begin to move more rapidly and take up more space. The filling begins to expand. At first the crust can contain the filling, even with the pressure building below. Finally, the pressure is enough to break through the crust

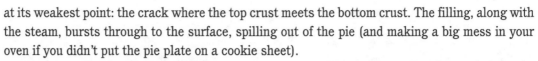

at its weakest point: the crack where the top crust meets the bottom crust. The filling, along with the steam, bursts through to the surface, spilling out of the pie (and making a big mess in your oven if you didn't put the pie plate on a cookie sheet).

When you take the pie out of the oven, look at its new shape. With less filling inside, the crust collapses into the pie, forming a deep, bowl-like shape. Compare this to the caldera boundary on your park map, extending about thirty miles north and south, and forty-five miles east and west. The events that created the Yellowstone caldera are very similar to what happened in your pie.

The Yellowstone hotspot lies about two miles below the surface of the earth. As the magma in that chamber heats, it expands, just like the pie filling (though the temperature has to be thousands of degrees hotter to melt rock). The earth's crust is fairly solid, like your piecrust, but it has weak spots. Geologically, the weak spots are faults and fractures caused by earthquakes, which form a ring pattern of cracks in the surface of the earth. When the pressure becomes too great for the magma chamber to hold, the molten rock leaks out of these weak spots in the crust. If the pressure is great enough, the magma may be released from many places at once, causing a violent, explosive eruption of lava and ash, such as the one that occurred in Yellowstone about 640,000 years ago.

With the magma gone (and the pie filling all over your oven), the chamber below is empty. The piecrust collapsed without the filling and so will the ground. All of the rocky peaks that may have extended from the Tetons into Yellowstone a couple million years ago collapsed into the giant hole left after the volcanic eruption. When the ash settled, the mountains were gone and a massive caldera remained.

If you wanted to keep your Caldera-Berry Pie from collapsing, you could have cut a few two-inch slits in the upper crust. These slits would have allowed the steam and pressure to escape gradually, preventing an explosion around the rim. It is doubtful that massive eruptions of the Yellowstone hotspot can be prevented in the same way, but the geologic record shows several small, pressure-releasing eruptions since the last major event. The west thumb of Yellowstone Lake, for example, is a small crater within the larger caldera, the result of an eruption about 150,000 years ago. Other lava flows have filled in the mound of rubble left when the caldera collapsed to create the navigable topography we drive around today.

Note: To eat your pie, spoon the escaped pie filling back into the pie (or on top of the crust). Cool slightly and serve with vanilla ice cream.

HUCKLEBERRY TUFF BREAKFAST BARS

As you explore Yellowstone National Park, you probably won't see active volcanoes oozing red-hot magma over the hills and forests. Though it has been at least 70,000 years since magma came to the surface at Yellowstone, the volcano has left its mark all over the park, particularly in the rocks.

Using essentially the same ingredients, a volcano creates dozens of types of rock by varying the cooling method. The superhot magma flows that swept over Yellowstone during the eruption of the hotspot spread a silica-rich rock called *rhyolite* throughout the area. Fast-moving pyroclastic flows of hot rock and gas left behind a darker color of rock than the slower rhyolitic flows that

followed the massive volcanic eruption. These silica-rich flows of rhyolite oozed over the landscape in a dough-like blob, filling in the cracks left by the volcanic explosion. Magma that cooled rapidly at the surface created the glassy rock known as *obsidian.* Ash that fell around the volcano hardened into the pumice-like rock called *tuff.*

Tuff begins as ash that is cast high into the air by the volcano. The ash is fine and smooth, but as it blasts through the crust it mixes with rocks along the way, falling back to the ground in a mess of rock and ash. The ash cements the bits of rock together, forming tuff.

Pick up a piece of tuff and look at it closely. Although it appears gray, it actually contains dozens of types of rock, each with its own shade and quality. Imagine the volcano blasting through layers of pink, black, and gray rock, blowing them up in the air, then settling into mounds of tuff. The ash holds the rock together as the corn syrup and peanut butter stick together these Huckleberry Tuff Breakfast Bars.

Huckleberry Tuff Breakfast Bars

½ cup sunflower seeds

¼ cup sesame seeds

¼ teaspoon salt

2 cups dried fruit (berries, cherries, apricots, raisins, dates, etc.)

½ cup white or semisweet chocolate chips

1 cup oatmeal

7 cups crisp rice cereal

1 cup light corn syrup

1 cup sugar

1 ½ cups peanut butter

1 cup powdered milk

1 teaspoon vanilla

1 teaspoon almond extract

Toast sunflower and sesame seeds in a dry skillet. Stir frequently until seeds turn light brown. Salt mixture and let cool.

Chop the dried fruit and chocolate chips into small pieces. You may use a food processor to combine ingredients by pulsing a few times. Combine this mixture, the seed mixture, and the cereal in a large bowl.

Combine corn syrup, sugar, and peanut butter in a microwave-safe container. Heat in microwave until the mixture begins to bubble. Stir until smooth. Add powdered milk, vanilla, and almond extract. Blend well.

Pour the liquid ingredients over the cereal mix and stir until evenly coated.

Grease a large jellyroll pan (10 x 15 inches) with butter. Coat hands with butter and scoop the energy bar mixture into the pan. Press evenly over the pan, filling in corners. Cut into squares, then allow to cool completely. Remove from pan and serve, or wrap in plastic wrap for the road or trail.

Look for Huckleberry Ridge tuff near Flagg Ranch, between Yellowstone National Park and Grand Teton National Park. At the ridge, this brown-to-purple colored rock is about 800 feet wide.

Glassy Obsidian Candy

During a volcanic eruption, much of the molten rock cools slowly underground, forming solid igneous rocks. The magma that flows to the surface cools at varying rates. If the magma encounters water on the surface or extreme atmospheric conditions, it cools very rapidly. This rapid, even cooling does not allow crystals to form, creating a glassy rock called *obsidian*. This sudden cooling method is the same technique used to give hard sugar candy a glassy appearance.

Glassy Obsidian Candy

2 cups sugar

½ cup light corn syrup

licorice-flavored oil

   (may substitute another flavor as desired)

½ cup water

black food coloring

Combine sugar, syrup, water, and a few drops of food coloring in a large saucepan (as the liquid heats it will foam and boil, so make sure your pot is big enough to allow the mixture to double in size). Bring the liquid to a boil over medium-high heat. Boil several minutes, without stirring, until the temperature reaches 300 degrees Fahrenheit, as measured on a candy thermometer.

Remove from heat. Let cool about 10 seconds.

Stir in up to 1 teaspoon flavored oil until blended. Carefully pour mixture onto a large plate or small cookie sheet (or onto a layer of powdered sugar spread on a tabletop covered with waxed paper). Let cool until hard, then "shatter" into bite-size pieces.

Gather together chunks of obsidian candy into a ribbon-tied bag, and enjoy a glassy rock treat that's a lot tastier to suck on than the real thing.

Note: For easier clean up, fill saucepan with warm, soapy water immediately after emptying.

Obsidian Cliff, located about halfway between Mammoth Hot Springs and Norris Junction, is the most famous obsidian feature in Yellowstone and possibly the world. Early accounts described a mountain made entirely of glass that sparkled in the sunlight. Today, many visitors drive right by black Obsidian Cliff, unless perhaps a boulder catches the sun just right. In the sun's rays, the obsidian glimmers to life, scattering light around the hillside over hundreds of boulders that have eroded from the face of the cliff. Due to extreme vandalism—millions of tourists pocketing pieces of shiny black rock as souvenirs—Obsidian Cliff is closed to foot travel, though you can still enjoy views of the glassy mountain from across the road. *Please do not remove rocks or other artifacts from Obsidian Cliff or anywhere in Yellowstone.*

Mammoth Springs Surprise

When I was ten years old, I decided to make my mom a special breakfast for Mother's Day. I got up early one morning, crept into the kitchen, and pulled a 3 × 5 card titled "Blueberry Muffins" from Mom's recipe file. I carefully measured the flour, sugar, baking powder, and salt, spooning each ingredient into a big mixing bowl. Meticulously following each step of the recipe, I stirred the batter, poured it into greased tins, and baked at 400 degrees. I perched on a stool where I could look at my muffins through the oven glass and counted the minutes until they were done. At last I pulled them from the oven and tipped them from the tins to cool. They looked so beautiful!

When I couldn't wait a moment longer, I slit a hot muffin in half, buttered it, and raised it to my mouth. That first taste was . . . awful! It didn't taste sweet and fruity at all, but had a strange, tangy flavor. My muffins were ruined and I couldn't figure out why. I was sure I had followed the recipe exactly. When Mom found me sobbing on the kitchen floor, she examined the mess of flour, eggs, and spices I'd left on the counter. Finally, she picked up a tiny bottle and held it next to the

ROCKS ON THE MOVE

In our day of refined steel, we may not appreciate the value of a sharp tool. Not too long ago, having a sharp tool was only possible if you could find one or fashion one from your natural environment. Thus a strong, rocklike obsidian was a prized possession. By carefully working the rock, causing it to fracture and break in precise places, Native Americans shaped obsidian into spearheads for killing animals, scrapers for skinning animals, and knives for cutting the meat.

For hundreds of years, Native Americans have come to Yellowstone for many reasons, practical and spiritual. Stopping by Obsidian Cliff was an important part of these historic Yellowstone journeys. Groups might spend a few days near the cliff, gathering rock and shaping it into the necessary tools. They also collected obsidian for trade. People who did not have their own sources of the treasured rock would eagerly trade with those who did.

The obsidian trade was extensive, and little pieces of rock from Yellowstone traveled all over the continent. Obsidian from Yellowstone has been found as far away as what is now southern Ohio.

recipe card. I compared the label on the bottle to the recipe and realized my mistake. I had substituted "cardamom," a spice for sauerkraut and stews, for "cinnamon." By putting in just half a teaspoon of the wrong ingredient, I had ruined the entire recipe.

Just as blueberry muffins need the right ingredients to come out looking and tasting as they should, places like Yellowstone are the result of certain "ingredients" coming together in the right quantities and for just the right amount of time. There are more geysers in Yellowstone National Park than anywhere else in the world because this region has just the right amount of four important ingredients: *heat, water, volcanic rocks,* and *earthquakes.* There are many places in the world that have two or three of the ingredients, but Yellowstone has the perfect proportion of all four.

Heat

The source of heat at Yellowstone is a 50-million-year-old volcano. A chamber of magma, called a hot spot, sits about two miles below the surface of the Yellowstone plateau. In comparison to the molten core of the earth, which is about 1,800 miles from the surface, that hot spot is quite close, and we feel its effects. The ground at Yellowstone, for example, is approximately 10 degrees warmer than the average ground temperature across the continent—in spite of the fact that it is covered with snow for six or more months every year. (To learn more about how the hotspot works, try making Caldera-Berry Pie.)

Water

When all that snow melts, it percolates into the ground where it becomes superheated. Compared to many places on the planet, Yellowstone gets very little water, about 10 inches per year in the north and up to 80 inches in the southwest. (In contrast, Mount Waialeale in Hawaii gets more than 450 inches of rain per year.) Geysers don't need very much water, but they obviously need some. More important than rainwater, however, is the water located underground and how it moves around in those superheated rocks.

Volcanic Rocks

The Yellowstone hot spot has had several violent volcanic eruptions over the past 16 million years, building up layer upon layer of rhyolite rock across the region. Most volcanoes deposit basaltic rock, which doesn't contain much silica, a hard mineral that is highly concentrated in rhyolitic rocks. As the magma superheats the underground water, the silica dissolves out of the rhyolite and flows to the surface, where it is redeposited as the hard rock *geyserite*—one of only a few rocks strong enough to withstand the enormous pressure of a geyser eruption. While most volcanoes around the world have hot springs nearby, without the right type of rock they cannot build a plumbing system for a geyser.

Earthquakes

Every time a geyser erupts, it deposits a little more silica along its plumbing system. Though the mineral builds up slowly, eventually the narrow cracks and fissures that channel the water become sealed up with silica and the geyser stops erupting. Fortunately, Yellowstone is one of the most active seismic regions in the world (a result of both its Rocky Mountain location and the huffing and puffing of the magma chamber underground). About 2,000 earthquakes a year rattle the ground around Yellowstone. Most of these quakes are not felt, but they keep the plumbing systems of Yellowstone's geysers open and flowing.

Absent any one of these ingredients—heat, water, rhyolite, earthquakes—Yellowstone would not have the spectacular geysers and hot springs (or even the waterfalls, canyons, rivers, lakes, vegetation, and wildlife) that make it famous. Furthermore, while the four key ingredients are common to the whole region, there is a great deal of geologic diversity within the park, rather like a variation on the same recipe. Yellowstone's dozens of strange and unique features are created from the same basic recipe, giving us lumpy mud pots, acidic geysers, or travertine terraces.

If you were to write a recipe for a geyser, using the four ingredients described above, what would it look like? Can you think about rocks and water the same way you think about flour and buttermilk in the kitchen? Below is my "recipe" for Mammoth Springs Surprise, describing how the travertine terraces at Mammoth Hot Springs were formed over a period of 500 million years. Notice that while Mammoth Hot Springs looks very different from geysers around Old Faithful, the four essential ingredients are still present.

Mammoth Springs Surprise

Preparation time: 500 million years

Ingredients: Water, travertine, cyanobacteria, and algae

Step 1: Pour up to 12 inland seas, one at a time, onto a large plate. Allow sediment to settle, then cover with thousands of feet of lava and ash. Let sit for 40 million years.

Step 2: Violently shake the plate until large cracks form in the crust.

Step 3: Move plate on top of heat source and heat to 500 degrees.

Step 4: Pour water over the surface. As the water heats it will cycle back to the surface. Voila! Mammoth Springs Surprise!

Step 5: Decorate with colorful bacteria and algae. Shake frequently.

Store in a national park. If stored properly, you can enjoy Mammoth Springs Surprise for many years.

Serves: Millions

Cost per serving: Priceless

STOVETOP GEYSERS

There are over 10,000 thermal features within the boundaries of Yellowstone National Park. No two of these features are exactly identical. In fact, features that look quite different from each other will often be found sitting side by side in a geyser basin. Still, all thermal features, whether they shoot water 200 feet in the air or ooze mud though a narrow vent, have three common ingredients: water, heat, and a plumbing system. Heat fuels all the thermal activity and water levels vary throughout the park, but the form a thermal feature has on the surface depends primarily on what's happening underground in its plumbing system.

In spite of their abundance and variety, all thermal features can be classed into four general categories: geysers, hot springs, fumaroles, and mud pots. The difference between these features lies in the plumbing system. Whether the hot water will reach the surface as a geyser or mud pot depends on the cracks and fissures that channel it to the surface.

EVERYDAY TRAVERTINE

Mammoth Hot Springs is essentially an enormous antacid tablet. Over two tons of a white, crumbly rock called travertine *are deposited throughout the Mammoth thermal system every day. Because Mammoth sits above an ancient limestone deposit, travertine has a different chemical composition than the siliceous sinter, or geyserite, found in other geyser basins. The soft (at least for a rock) quality of travertine cannot handle the amount of pressure necessary for a geyser eruption, which is why Mammoth forms its remarkable terrace formations instead becoming a "typical" geyser field.*

Travertine is primarily composed of calcium carbonate, an ingredient found in a variety of household products. Check the labels of the following common items to see if you're nibbling on or scrubbing with bits of travertine.

Toothpaste	*White paint*
Stomach antacids	*Shoe polish*
Vitamin and mineral supplements	*Caulking*
Chalk	*Carpet backing*
Bathroom cleaner	

To create your own stovetop thermal systems, gather together a large pot or saucepan, a teakettle, and a pressure cooker. Fill each container with water and place on the stove. Turn each burner to its highest setting and watch the water as it heats.

Saucepan Springs

Watch the water in the saucepan (do not cover with a lid). Heat transfers to the water through the pan in a *conduction* current. On your stove, the heat source is the electric burner or gas flame; the heat source for Yellowstone's hot springs is magma found below the earth's surface. That magma heats the rocks above it, which transfer heat to the water by conduction.

Each container on your stove will heat the water differently, but certain principles will remain consistent no matter what shape the pan is. Hot water tries to rise above cooler water. This is true on your stove and it is also true in Yellowstone. As water temperature increases, the individual water molecules become agitated and begin to move rapidly. These excited molecules take up more space than calmer, cooler water molecules, making the hot water less dense. Thus the lighter water floats to the surface. At the surface, air contacts and cools the water. Those agitated molecules slow their movement, condensing the water again and causing it to sink. As it approaches the heat source, the water heats and rises again, repeating the cycle. This circulating water, called a *convection* current, continuously moves water around the container.

As the water in your saucepan heats, bubbles begin to creep up the sides of the pan. These bubbles are water molecules that have been heated past the boiling point and have turned to steam. They float to the surface, where they can expand into the atmosphere and float away. The rising bubbles become bigger and more frequent as more water nears boiling temperature. Eventually the bubbles at the surface appear rapidly as more and more steam escapes through the water. We call this the boiling point.

Most of the hot springs in Yellowstone don't reach boiling temperature at the surface. Bubbling occurs in the pools as steam and gas escape from lower depths. The convection current keeps the water circulating below the boiling point, slightly cooler at the surface where the water contacts the atmosphere and cools. Like your saucepan, a hot spring has an open, unrestricted plumbing system that allows this convection current to move the water freely about.

Steam Vent in a Kettle

We always know when water is hot for tea because the kettle starts to whistle. A thermal feature that whistles like a teakettle is called a *fumarole,* or steam vent. When the teakettle on your stove starts to whistle, look at the opening making all the noise. Steam pushes through the narrow opening so rapidly that it shrieks as it passes through. The water you put in the kettle, however, is not coming out the hole—at least not in liquid form. Deep inside, the water boils and turns to steam, expanding and escaping through that very narrow opening.

The water in a fumarole system also lies well below the surface. The boiling water sends steam up through a narrow opening where it comes to the surface as a white, cloudy mist. Some fumaroles hiss gently, while others gush clouds of vapor. If the opening is narrow enough, a fumarole will whistle like a teakettle as the steam escapes at the surface.

Pressure-Cooking Geysers

A very narrow constriction near the surface distinguishes a geyser from a hot spring. Constrictions limit the ability of liquid to travel through an opening. Imagine that someone has clamped her hands around your neck, squeezing your throat. You can't swallow or cough because the pressure from the hands restricts the movement of liquids in your throat. This is a constriction.

In the saucepan, steam was able to escape freely. In a pressure cooker, a very narrow opening traps steam in the pan. The gauge on the pressure cooker holds in pressure, allowing the water to become superheated. (When you cook potatoes in your pressure cooker, they cook faster because the water is hotter. The pressure cooker increases the boiling point of the water, so it stays in liquid phase longer. Hotter water means faster cooking.) Now the stove can heat the water much beyond the boiling point.

What would happen if you removed the pressure gauge? Steam and water would push through that narrow opening as the unpressurized water flashed to steam. (Because that pressure can be intense enough to burst the metal of the pan, remove the pan from the heat and *let it cool for several minutes before attempting to release the pressure*.) The intense pressure built up by expanding steam would be enough to force both water and steam through that tiny opening and "erupt" all over your stove.

Making a Mud Pot?

So, how would you go about making a mud pot on the stove? The plumbing system of a mud pot is similar to a hot spring, and as they dry up mud pots will often turn to fumaroles. The key to a mud pot actually lies in the water chemistry. Mud pots are acidic, with a pH level roughly the same as battery acid. The water coming to the surface is so acidic it can actually dissolve solid rock. The grains of rock, water from below, and water from rain and snow mix together to form a gooey mud, which clogs up the opening of the spring. Now, in order for gasses to escape, they have to push through the mud, causing it to glop and plop all over the place, even shooting mud several feet into the air. If you try to make a mud pot on your stove, you'd better be prepared to clean up a mess!

BISCUIT BASIN BISCUITS

Thousands of thermal features in Yellowstone are grouped together into geyser basins. The term "basin" comes from the bowl-like appearance of many of these geyser groups. The basin concept is geologically sound, as thermal activity tends to occur in natural valleys where water collects to supply the geyser systems. These are topographical basins.

The largest geyser basin in Yellowstone is the Upper Geyser Basin, home of Old Faithful geyser and about 200 others. Technically, Black Sand Basin and Biscuit Basin are part of the same system that forms the Upper Geyser Basin, though they have their own names and parking areas. About 20 percent of the world's geysers are found in the one and a half square miles of Upper Geyser Basin. The two other basins along the Firehole River are called Midway and Lower Basin, for their respective positions along that river, which flows from south to north through the park.

Biscuit Basin gets its name for biscuit-shaped silica deposits that once scattered the basin. These geyserite rocks are no longer visible in the basin, due either to vandalism or to an increase in runoff from Sapphire Spring washing them into the Firehole River.

Biscuit Basin Biscuits

2 cups flour	½ teaspoon salt
½ cup sugar	½ cup butter, softened
3 teaspoons baking powder	¾ cup buttermilk

Preheat oven to 450 degrees. Mix flour, sugar, baking powder, and salt until combined. Using two forks, cut in softened butter. Work together using forks until lumps of butter are about the size of peas. Add milk slowly while stirring. Mix well. If necessary, add more flour until dough takes shape. Dough should still be quite sticky. Drop big spoonfuls onto an ungreased cookie sheet. Bake 9 to 12 minutes, until the tops are golden brown.

SODA FAITHFUL

Have you ever popped the lid of a soda can, and had the sticky liquid come gushing out in a geyser-like explosion? That's because the "plumbing" of your soda can is similar to the plumbing of a geyser.

In the early 1990s geologists lowered a camera down the center of Old Faithful geyser (they had to time it so the camera didn't melt in the hot, hot water of the geyser). About twenty-five feet below

Old Faithful's rim, they found an opening just four inches wide. Below the narrow opening, the camera saw two chambers of water, the first about the size of an automobile, the second no larger than a bus. When Old Faithful erupts, in as little as two minutes, thousands of gallons of water from the chambers roar through that crack no wider than your palm! The most basic geyser plumbing system needs little more than a reservoir of water with a narrow opening—kind of like a can of soda.

So what makes the soda erupt? When soda is carbonated, the liquid is infused with gases. While the can sits on your shelf, the little bubbles of gas float to the top, where they can easily escape when you pop the tab. By shaking the can, however, you mix those gas bubbles back into the liquid. This time, when you open the can, the gases must push the liquid out of the way, forcing it out the opening and all over the floor.

Now visualize the plumbing system of Old Faithful in terms of your can of soda. The rhyolite-coated chambers slowly fill with water fed from the ground. The water heats, eventually reaching the boiling point; it can no longer exist as a liquid and turns to steam. Water in the gas phase needs more space than water in the liquid phase: a shoebox of water, if boiled, would produce enough steam to fill an entire railroad boxcar. The water in the plumbing system of these geysers gets superheated before it turns to gas because the extreme pressure from the overlying rock increases the boiling temperature. The narrow constriction and water already in the system act like a plug, keeping the pressure high. Some geologists estimate that the water can be as hot as 800 degrees Fahrenheit before it starts to boil.

Eventually, however, some of the water begins to boil. As the water at the bottom of the chamber boils, steam bubbles climb toward the top, seeking a way out of the system. The first few bubbles easily escape, but as more and more steam forms they fight against each other for space. Like the bubbles in the can of soda, the gases in the geyser must push the water out of the way in order to escape from the chamber. This pulls the geyser's "plug," releasing pressure the same way you did when you popped the top of the soda can. Suddenly the water, which was not boiling because it was held under pressure, flashes to steam. There is no escape except through that narrow opening. In its effort to expand, the steam has enough power to force gallons of not-yet-boiling water through that tiny hole and hundreds of feet in the air.

When the chambers have emptied much of their water and the pressure has subsided, the eruption stops. All is quiet as the chambers begin to fill and heat again, preparing for the next eruption. And if there's some soda left in your can, you can go ahead and drink it.

It Smells Like Rotten Eggs . . .

All around the boardwalks of Yellowstone you will meet people holding their noses to block out the smell of "rotten eggs." While you boil eggs for Not-So-Rotten Egg Salad, breathe deeply, think of Yellowstone, and consider these egg-citing facts about Yellowstone:

🌿 The "rotten egg" smell at Yellowstone comes from hydrogen sulfide gas (H_2S). Hydrogen sulfide can be smelled even in very small amounts. Most of the gasses you see rising out of geysers and hot springs are steam (H_2O) and carbon dioxide (CO_2), but that pinch of hydrogen sulfide is enough to make it smell bad.

BUT THIS DOESN'T LOOK LIKE A VOLCANO . . .

Hot spots—pools of molten rock close to the surface of the earth—are among the most interesting geologic features on the planet. The Yellowstone volcano is unique among hot spots because here the magma pushes through a thick continental crust, which can be more than 40 miles thick. Most volcanoes develop along oceanic plates, which are relatively thin, perhaps just three miles thick. Volcanism is not unusual along oceanic plates, or at the edges where two plates collide, but it is unusual for magma to push so close to the surface right in the middle of a continent. Consequently, when the Yellowstone hotspot erupts, it looks different from other volcanoes.

In addition to massive lava flows, the Yellowstone volcano spews out millions of tons of volcanic ash. One eruption of the hotspot can bury the entire state of Wyoming in 38 feet of ash! The ash is also carried by the wind and deposited hundreds of miles from the volcanic center. Because every volcanic explosion creates a mixture of rock and mineral unique to that particular eruption, by comparing the mineral "ingredients" of volcanic rocks around the country, geologists can determine which volcano deposited each layer of rock and when. Ash from the last three eruptions of the Yellowstone hotspot has been found as far away as Texas, Nebraska, and Southern California.

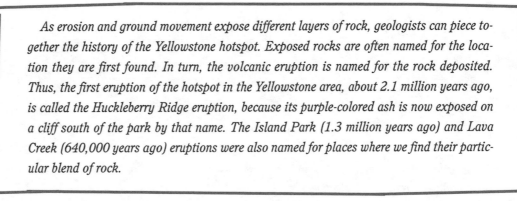

As erosion and ground movement expose different layers of rock, geologists can piece together the history of the Yellowstone hotspot. Exposed rocks are often named for the location they are first found. In turn, the volcanic eruption is named for the rock deposited. Thus, the first eruption of the hotspot in the Yellowstone area, about 2.1 million years ago, is called the Huckleberry Ridge eruption, because its purple-colored ash is now exposed on a cliff south of the park by that name. The Island Park (1.3 million years ago) and Lava Creek (640,000 years ago) eruptions were also named for places where we find their particular blend of rock.

🐾 Hydrogen sulfide gas is toxic, but not in the amounts you are likely to breathe in the park. H_2S can be picked up by our noses at a concentration of just 1 or 2 parts per million, which is about the amount found in Yellowstone's hot springs. If you breathe in gas with a concentration of more than 30 ppm, you may begin to feel nauseous or develop a headache. At extremely high levels (more than 300 ppm), you will no longer be able to smell the hydrogen sulfide because it dulls your olfactory glands. At these levels it can be fatal.

🐾 H_2S is rarely fatal in Yellowstone because the atmosphere continuously circulates gases, preventing hydrogen sulfide from building up a high enough concentration to be deadly. On rare occasions, gases do accumulate in lethal amounts. Death Gulch, a narrow gully in the Lamar River valley, earned its name in 1889 when several carcasses, including six grizzly and some elk, were found piled up in its bottom. A cave feature near Mammoth, the Devil's Kitchen, was closed when gases were detected inside the windless cavern. In March 2004, five bison were found dead in the Norris Geyser Basin when a temperature inversion on a cold day trapped hydrogen sulfide, which is heavier than air, near the ground allowing it to build up to deadly levels. To avoid hydrogen sulfide poisoning in Yellowstone, be wary of confined areas that do not allow the air to circulate. Remember, as long as you can smell the "rotten eggs" you should be safe.

 A microbiotic organism called *Sulfolobus* can be found in some hot springs, particularly around the Norris Geyser Basin and Mud Volcano. This single-celled prokaryotic organism draws energy by "eating" sulfur. After dinner it "burps" out sulfuric acid and hydrogen sulfide gas, making the water in these areas very acidic.

  It will take you longer to boil your egg if you are cooking at a high altitude. The Yellowstone plateau has been pushed up to an elevation about 8,000 feet above sea level. With less atmosphere weighing down on the water, the boiling point decreases to about 200 degrees Fahrenheit. At sea level, with all that extra atmospheric pressure, the boiling point is 212 degres Fahrenheit. Once water hits the boiling point it turns to steam, so your pot can never get much hotter than 200 degrees if you're cooking at Yellowstone. With a little less heat it takes longer to cook that egg.

  In Japan, eggs boiled in hot springs are eaten for good luck. While cooking in the hot water, the eggs turn colorful shades of black and purple. Hot springs in Yellowstone could be used for

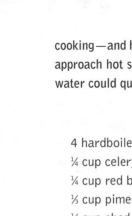

cooking—and have been historically—but it is illegal to do so today. Not only is it dangerous to approach hot springs close enough to toss in an egg, but traces of mercury and arsenic in the water could quickly turn your dinner into something much more dangerous.

Not-So-Rotten Egg Salad

4 hardboiled eggs

¼ cup celery, finely chopped

¼ cup red bell pepper, chopped

⅓ cup pimento-stuffed green olives, chopped

¼ cup cheddar cheese, shredded

2 tablespoons fresh basil, chopped

1 tablespoon dill weed, chopped

3 tablespoons mayonnaise

pinch cayenne pepper

dash seasoned salt

Boil, shell, and slice the eggs. Combine eggs with all other ingredients, mixing well. Season with cayenne and seasoned salt to taste. Refrigerate until chilled.

Serve on bread, with crackers, or as a side salad.

SODA MACHINE

It is illegal and unwise to drink from any of the thermal springs in Yellowstone National Park, though names like Soda Springs and Punch Bowl Spring promise a refreshing drink. As early as 1830 trappers told tales of a "soda spring" near present-day Mammoth Hot Springs. A spring in the area, which bears the name today, was cleaned out in the 1880s and shaped with boards to make it easier to fill bottles from the spring. This feature was used this way into the 1940s, though now it is little more than a shallow, grassy depression.

Another feature in the Lamar River Valley bears the name Soda Butte. An 1879 visitor who sought to quench his thirst in these soda waters met with an unpleasant reward. As he later wrote:

> I do not distinctly recall all the nasty tastes which have afflicted my palate, but I am quite sure this was one of the vilest. It was a combination of acid, sulphur, and saline, like a diabolic julep of lucifer matches, bad eggs, vinegar, and magnesia. I presume its horrible taste has secured it a reputation for being good when it is down.[1]

Perhaps sweetening the water up with a little sugar and a few fresh berries would have helped the soda go down.

Yellowstone-Sweetened Soda

2 pounds ripe berries (raspberries, blueberries, strawberries)
1 quart carbonated water
sugar to taste

Warm berries slightly by microwaving in a large bowl about 1 minute. Remove from microwave and mash well (with a fork or potato masher). Pour berry mixture into a strainer, catching the juice in another bowl. Work pulp slightly with masher to extract as much juice as possible. Save berry pulp, if desired, for use in another recipe or to eat plain.

Add a bit of sugar to berry juice if desired, particularly if using tart berries. Pour in carbonated water and mix well. Drop in a few ice cubes to chill and serve.

ORANGE SPRING MOUND SUNDAES

After walking around a geyser basin for a few hours, being baked by the sun above and cooked from the ground below, it's easy to start imagining things in the shape of the hot springs. A trip to Orange Spring Mound on such a day will immediately trigger a craving for an ice cream sundae. This travertine cone, found on the upper terraces of Mammoth Hot Springs, oozes water from a narrow crack at the top of the mound. As the water slips down the sides, bacteria and algae coat the rock, creating a swirl of creamy orange and brown over a scoop of white rock. With a homemade butterscotch topping, these ice cream sundaes will cool off even the strongest geyser-induced craving.

Orange Spring Mound Sundaes

Vanilla ice cream	Whipped cream
Butterscotch topping (below)	Nuts, if desired

Prepare butterscotch filling as directed below.

Scoop ice cream into serving dishes. Ladle with butterscotch topping. Top with a dollop of whipped cream and sprinkle with nuts. Serve immediately.

Butterscotch Topping

1 cup brown sugar

⅔ cup light corn syrup

¼ cup butter

⅔ cup cream

⅛ teaspoon baking soda

1 teaspoon vanilla

In a medium saucepan, combine sugar, syrup, and butter. Cook over medium heat, stirring constantly, until mixture comes to a boil. Let boil one minute without stirring. Remove from heat.

In a large measuring cup, combine cream, soda, and vanilla. Stir until blended, then pour into sugar mixture. Serve warm over scoops of vanilla ice cream, or pour into jars to store in the refrigerator.

MORNING GLORY MOLDED SALAD

Can you imagine living in a pool of nearly boiling water? Or a pit of acid with a pH about like battery acid? Or perhaps a pool of boiling acid? Not only are there organisms in Yellowstone that can survive in these conditions, but there are billions of microorganisms that actually *thrive* in the hot, often acidic, geysers and hot springs of Yellowstone. They go by different names: *thermophile*, for the heat-loving organisms ("thermo" for heat, "phile" for lover), *extremophile*, for those that love extreme heat, and *thermoacidophile*, for an organism that loves acidity as well as heat. These organisms grow in communities, often with many different species, each displaying a different color or shape on the surface.

These microorganisms survive under conditions that would be quickly fatal for humans. Some photosynthesize, while others chemosynthesize, drawing energy from chemicals in the rock and water. Some organisms have learned to exist without light. Some are able to repair their own DNA, a defense against acidic waters which constantly eat away at them. Some insects have even adapted to the warm runoff channels where they can survive through the cold Yellowstone winter.

It takes a powerful microscope to see individual thermophilic organisms, but since they conglomerate in large communities, we can identify them by their colors and shapes on the surface. Different temperatures and acidities allow different types of organisms to survive. Thus, the appearance of the microorganisms tells something about the quality of the water as well.

Many hot springs in Yellowstone have rings of color. The different colors mark changes in the water conditions, causing a shift in the types of organisms that can grow there. At the center of a hot spring, where the temperature is the hottest, only the most heat-tolerant organisms can survive. Often, these are colorless bacteria and other single-celled organisms called archaea. Thus, the center of the pool looks blue, like swimming pool water looks blue when lined with white tiles. The edges of the pool are cooler, allowing different organisms to survive, often in shades of yellow and orange. In the runoff channels and around the very shallow edges of a pool, the temperature drops enough that algae can grow, giving the pool a dark rim of green and black.

Morning Glory Pool is one of the most famous hot springs in Yellowstone. Some visitors remember driving right up to the delicately colored pool as they entered the Upper Geyser Basin, home of Old Faithful geyser. Today, the main park road has been routed around the geyser basin to protect fragile thermal features. Morning Glory is only accessible by a one-mile trail leaving from the Old Faithful Inn and Visitor Center. Those who do walk out to Morning Glory may also be surprised by changes in the pool's appearance. To many people, the pool looks different than they remember. The very hot temperature of the spring in the past allowed only the most heat-tolerant organisms to survive, giving the cornucopia-shaped pool just a dainty tint of pale blue color stretching to the depth of the pool. Today, the water temperature has dropped, allowing strains of orange and yellow cyanobacteria to creep down the shell of the pool. Temperatures in a spring naturally shift due to changes in the underground plumbing system. Changes in temperature create new environments, causing some microorganisms to die out while allowing other organisms to move into a new, hospitable space. Our eyes pick up on such shifts in water quality by observing the changing colors in the bacteria.

In Morning Glory Pool, however, humans caused the changes in color. For the sake of curiosity, experimentation, or even superstition, people have been tossing things into hot springs for decades. These objects, no matter how small, easily clog the narrow plumbing systems of geysers or hot springs. Because of its popularity and early proximity to the road, Morning Glory Pool has been the receptacle of thousands of foreign objects. Such items are clogging Morning Glory's plumbing system, slowing the circulation of water, and lowering the temperature of the Pool. Knowing that Morning Glory had erupted as a geyser at least once in its past, in 1950 the National Park Service forced an eruption of the pool by pumping water into the plumbing system. With the water emptied, the crater could be cleaned. The removed objects create an astounding collection: handkerchiefs, cans, clothes (socks, shirts, and even bras), and over $90 in coins—including more than 8,500 pennies.

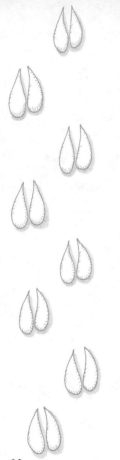

Subsequent attempts to force an eruption for "Spring Cleaning" have been unsuccessful. Though the road has been rerouted, Morning Glory still provides a tempting wishing well for many visitors. In the spring of 2004, a volunteer worked from the edge of the pool to remove another 2,800 coins from Morning Glory Pool, along with dozens of other objects including a medal, a bullet shell, and foreign coins. Many of these objects were coated in mineral, suggesting that they had been sitting in the pool for several years. Although people seem to be learning how destructive a simple act like tossing a penny can be, our presence threatens the future of all of Yellowstone's thermal features. While the sculpted opening and crystal blue waters of Morning Glory Pool are still a beautiful sight, and the hardy bacteria still paint it lovely shades of blue, green, yellow and orange, the spring can only return to its original glory if we keep our coins in our pockets and rocks on the ground.

Morning Glory Molded Salad

1 3-ounce package gelatin, lime flavor

1 3-ounce package gelatin, orange flavor

1 3-ounce package gelatin, blueberry or blue-raspberry flavor

fruit mix-ins as desired

water

whipped cream

To make this molded salad you will need three stackable bowls. The bowls should sit inside each other with at least an inch of space in between. You might use a large salad bowl (14-inch diameter), a mixing bowl (10- to 12-inch diameter), and a small mixing bowl (6- to 8-inch diameter). It is convenient, but not necessary, if all three are roughly the same height.

Prepare lime gelatin according to directions on package, using a little less water than directed (reduce by 3 to 4 tablespoons). Pour into largest bowl and chill slightly, but not until set. Lightly oil the outside of the medium-size bowl, using oil or nonstick cooking spray. Place mid-size bowl in the larger bowl and press down until the gelatin rises up around the edges of the bowl. Hold middle bowl down by setting a heavy object, such as a can of food, inside the middle bowl. Return to refrigerator and chill until firm.

Prepare orange gelatin as directed, again with slightly less water, and chill in saucepan to thicken. When lime gelatin is set, remove from refrigerator. Pull out middle-size bowl (if it sticks to the gelatin, try warming the bowl with a kitchen cloth or hot water). Pour about half of the orange gelatin into the bowl shape left in the lime gelatin. Place the small bowl in the center of the ring and push down slightly. Watch as the level of the orange gelatin rises around the sides of the bowl. You want to match the level of the orange gelatin to the lime gelatin. When the small bowl is pushed and weighted down, spoon additional orange gelatin into the mold to raise the level to the same depth as the lime gelatin. Carefully move to the refrigerator and chill until firm.

Prepare blueberry or blue raspberry gelatin as directed on the package. Chill gelatin until cool but not set. When the orange gelatin is firm, remove the bowls from the refrigerator. Carefully remove the inner bowl, warming the edges if necessary to lift it from the gelatin. Pour blue gelatin into the hole left behind by the small bowl. Add just enough gelatin to be level with the orange and lime layers. (Excess gelatin may be poured into a small cake pan or other mold to be chilled separately.) Return the gelatin to the refrigerator and chill until the entire salad is firm.

HOW DO YOU CLEAN A GEYSER?

With such a limited market for geyser maintenance supplies, there aren't many companies out there making equipment for cleaning out geysers. Yellowstone employees have had to come up with their own tools for removing foreign objects from the park's thermal features. Fortunately, many items found right in your kitchen work great for cleaning up geysers. A metal slotted spoon, lashed to the end of a long pole (using duct tape, of course), can be used to scoop up small items like rocks and pennies. One side of a salad tong can also be lashed to a pole in order to scrape up items clinging to the edges. Ice picks on sticks work well for retrieving hats, though your cap might have a little hole in it should you want it back. Scrub brushes are also used to wipe away graffiti scribbled in the bacteria mats of the runoff channels. Park rangers don't like having to scrub away billions of microorganisms to wipe out someone's name, but they want park visitors to be able to enjoy these features in their most natural state—without someone's name or pocket change marring the view.

Serve with whipped cream around the edges like little mounds of geyserite.

Note: Fruit or other mix-ins can be added to any of the layers as desired. For the most authentic look, try adding grated cucumber to the green (algae) layer, shredded carrots to the orange (bacteria) layer, and coconut to simulate white, filamentous bacteria in the center of the pool.

NOTE

1. *Lippincott's Magazine,* July 1880, 33.

Chapter Two
Wildlife

hough Yellowstone National Park was created to protect the fantastic geysers and hot springs, as the park matured it was soon evident that Yellowstone served as a haven for diverse forms of wildlife whose habitat was threatened by the settlement of the western frontier. Today, seeing bison, bears, and even wolves is a goal of most visitors to the national park. After enjoying the show at Old Faithful, they turn to the ranger without pause and ask, "Where can I go to see wildlife?"

With elk, bison, bears, and wolves roaming the park, most people won't be disappointed in their quest to spot wildlife. The eerie echo of a wolf howl or a glimpse of a stray tuft of bison fur rubbed off on a tree reward those who use all their senses to find the signs animals leave behind. Learning about animal behaviors before coming into the park increases the odds that you will catch a glimpse of some of Yellowstone's more elusive wildlife. Summer months are busy eating times for Yellowstone's animals, who must build up reserves of food and calories in order to survive seven or eight months of snowy weather each year. If you look for the animal where it's likely to find food, you're more likely to find the animal.

GINGERBREAD FOOTPRINTS

Most people who visit Yellowstone hope to see two things: Old Faithful geyser and a bear. With eruptions every ninety minutes, Old Faithful is pretty much a guarantee, but if your luck's like mine, by the time you get to the front of the traffic jam, the bear will have sauntered back into the woods out of sight. Fortunately, with 20,000 elk, over 4,000 bison, hundreds of coyotes, and now almost 200 wolves, wildlife watchers are likely to be satisfied even without encountering the elusive grizzly.

On those hot summer days when the animals rest in the cool forest, safely hidden from sight, there are still many ways to enjoy Yellowstone's wildlife. The tracks and trails of Yellowstone's wildlife tell the animals' stories long after they have moved on. Make Gingerbread Footprints in your kitchen to learn the tracks to look for when you're out on the trail.

Gingerbread Footprints

Lay a piece of thin tracing paper over one of the tracks on the following pages. Trace the outline of that track with a dark pen or marker. Cut out shape. If you want to make several cookies of the same track, you may want to make a sturdier cardboard stencil. Lay the cutout track on a piece of clean cardboard, such as an old cereal box. Trace the outside of the track onto the cardboard, then cut the shape out of the cardboard. Write the letter of the track piece on the cardboard stencil, and save for later use.

¾ cup margarine

1 cup sugar

4 teaspoons baking powder

5 cups all-purpose flour

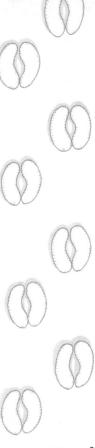

1 cup molasses	2 teaspoons ground cinnamon
2 eggs	1 teaspoon ground cloves
¼ cup cold water	1 ½ teaspoon ginger
1 teaspoon baking soda	½ teaspoon salt

Cream margarine, sugar, and molasses in large mixing bowl. Add eggs and water and mix well.

Sift together flour, soda, powder, salt, and spices (cinnamon, cloves, and ginger). Add to butter mixture and blend well. Dough should be sticky. Add up to ½ cup flour if needed to make more manageable.

Divide dough into four balls, slightly flattened. Wrap each disc in plastic wrap and refrigerate overnight (dough can be refrigerated up to 3 days).

Preheat oven to 350 degrees. Roll each portion of dough on a floured surface. Dough will be soft and sticky, so work quickly and use lots of flour. Dough should be ⅛ to ¼ inch thick.

Place your stencil on top of the rolled gingerbread dough and cut around the edges with a knife. If instructed, flip the paper stencil over and cut a mirror image of the shape. Gently lift each track with your fingers or a spatula. Place each part of the track on a greased cookie sheet.

Bake on greased cookie sheet for 10 minutes, until light and puffy. Remove from cookie sheet and cool.

When the cookie pieces are cool, spread a large sheet of waxed paper over your table. Using the chart and templates on pages 39–42, assemble your Yellowstone tracks.

To make . . .

pronghorn tracks trace one **A**, then flip it over and trace a mirror image

 **elk tracks B** and mirror image of **B**

bison tracks C and mirror image of **C**

 moose tracks D and mirror image of **D**

bighorn tracks E and mirror image of **E**

 **deer tracks F** and mirror image of **F**

wolf tracks **G**, four **J**, and four **M**

coyote tracks **H**, four **K**, and four **M**

 bobcat tracks **I** and four **K**

mountain lion tracks **L** and four **J**

bear tracks (front paw) one **N**, five **J**, and five **M**

bear tracks (rear paw) one **O**, five **J**, and five **M**

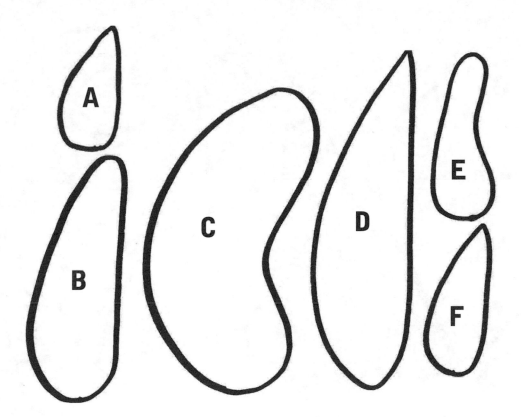

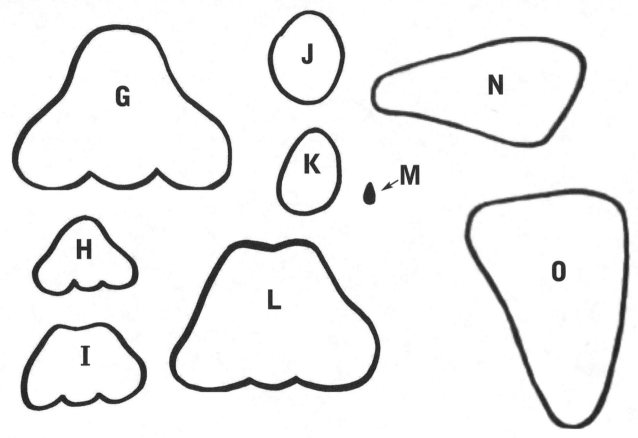

G

J

N

H

K

M

I

L

O

The Complete Chocolate Guide to Scat

(Warning: Do not read while eating *anything* chocolate!)

Learning to identify animal tracks and trails can be a daunting task, particularly since Yellowstone is home to sixty-one species of mammals, not to mention all the birds and reptiles. Plus, many tracks and scats (a fancy name for droppings) look similar to each other, particularly within the same animal families. Here's one handy—and unforgettable—way to distinguish between the scat of the *ungulates* (grass-eating animals like deer and elk).

For a visual reference, gather together a handful of chocolate chips, candy kisses, and chocolate eggs (the foil-wrapped kind often sold in the springtime).

Chocolate chips: Look at the chocolate chips. They are small, less than one-half inch long. One end is pointed, the other end is blunt. This is like *deer* scat. Deer scat will often be hard (from eating lots of dry grasses), "nippled" on one end and "dimpled" on the other, and found in piles about the size of a large handful of chocolate chips.

Candy kisses: A chocolate kiss is about the same size and shape of *elk* scat. Elk scat is much the same shape as deer scat, but larger (which makes sense, as a bull elk can weigh up to 700 pounds, while deer usually weigh less than 200 pounds). Elk eat a lot more food. Fresh elk scat will be darker than milk chocolate in color. It gets lighter brown as it gets older. Like a chocolate kiss, there will often be a point on one end of the scat, though it gets less distinct as the grasses elk eat get drier in late summer.

Chocolate eggs: The largest animal in the family Cervidae is the *moose.* A dry, woody diet makes moose scat lose the point that characterizes the scat of the smaller ungulates. Instead, the scat is

round and smooth, like a chocolate egg, and roughly the same size. Adult moose often weigh in around 1,000 pounds, so their scat is large. Also look for specks of wood and twigs in the scat.

There are other food tricks for learning scat, too. *Pronghorn antelope* scat looks a bit like deer scat, but it tends to clump together a little more, as if you had held chocolate chips in your hot hand too long.

Cat and dog scat (coyotes and wolves, cougars, and bobcats in Yellowstone) comes out like linked sausage. *Coyote* scat, which is generally no larger than breakfast sausage, is smaller than *wolf* scat, which can be the thickness of a hot dog. Similarly, *bobcat* scat is smaller than *cougar*. The last link of sausage, if it is dog scat, will have a pointed, slightly curled "tail." Cat links are blunt and broken up, and may be buried.

Try the following recipe for buffalo chips to learn how to read a bison scat.

Chewy Chocolaty Buffalo Chips

Bison scat, like the scat of any mammal, changes appearance depending on what the bison has been eating. Watch how these chocolate buffalo chips (a common name for bison scat) change appearance as you add new ingredients.

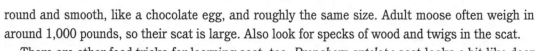

Chewy Chocolaty Buffalo Chips

⅓ cup coconut

1 3-ounce package lime gelatin

½ cup walnuts

4 tablespoons cocoa

1 cup hot water
3 cups oatmeal
¾ cup peanut butter

2 cups sugar
½ cup milk
1 cube (½ cup) margarine

In a small bowl, dissolve gelatin in the hot water. Add coconut and stir. Set aside.

In a medium-size saucepan, combine sugar, milk, and margarine. Stir over medium heat until margarine is melted. Add cocoa and stir until mixture comes to a boil. Let boil one minute and then remove from heat.

Add peanut butter and stir until blended. Add oatmeal and walnuts. Using two spoons, drop three marble-size lumps, one on top of another, on a sheet of waxed paper. Press lumps together slightly with the back of your spoon. Continue to drop in groups of three until half of the batter remains.

Using a colander or slotted spoon, strain coconut from gelatin. (If desired, you can add one cup cold water to the strained gelatin and refrigerate according to directions on package.) Drop the coconut onto a stack of two or three paper towels to drain. The coconut should now be dyed green.

Add the green coconut to the remaining batter along with one tablespoon milk and mix.

Drop golf ball–size lumps of the "grassy batter" onto waxed paper until all of the batter has been used. You may wish to further flatten the "patties" using the flat end of a glass.

When cookies have cooled, serve your Chewy Chocolaty Buffalo Chips to your most adventure-some friends. While they're chomping away, you can tell them these facts about bison scat:

- In the springtime, moist, green plants make moist, green buffalo chips. A fresh "patty" can be more than a foot in diameter.

- As grasses get drier at the end of summer and during the fall, bison scat also gets drier. Without the wet grass, the scat looks different. Wintertime buffalo scat looks like a can of re-frigerated biscuits when they pop out of the can into a pile of patties. One buffalo chip may look like several separate layers stacked on top of each other, giving a "corded" effect.

- Buffalo chips, when large and dry, burn very well. Western pioneers gathered buffalo chips to fuel their fires while crossing the great plains. Toss a buffalo patty into the fire the next time you're making s'mores, and see if they taste different.

Noodle Nests

By reading the tracks and scats you see on the trails in Yellowstone, you will begin to learn the stories animals silently tell as they fight to survive in the Yellowstone wilderness. Their tracks tell us where they are going and how quickly they are trying to get there. Their scat tells us what they've had to eat along the way. But there are many other signs that complete the story. A bare spot on a tree, for example, might tell of a hungry bison, unable to find any grasses under the snow, who resorted to pulling off bark to eat the juicy cambium layer below. A shredded tree sapling tells us that perhaps a bull elk rubbed off the velvety skin that covered his antlers while they grew all summer. And four or five long, parallel scratches on a tree says that a bear came through here marking its territory or maybe looking for a sticky, sappy backscratcher.

Seeing signs of elk, bison, and bears can be an exciting part of a hike through Yellowstone. But a keen eye will catch signs of many other animals as well. Beaver dams and muskrat lodges can been seen in streams and ponds throughout the park. Holes in the ground are homes for rodents like the Uinta ground squirrel. These squirrels are often mistaken for prairie dogs because both animals live in colonies and stand on their hind legs to survey the ground around them.

Don't forget to look up while you're tracking. More than 300 species of birds have summer homes in Yellowstone. Many of these birds are just stopping by in Yellowstone during long migrations, but about 150 types of birds are known to nest in the park. Some birds, such as ravens, are able to survive the cold temperatures of winter in Yellowstone and stay here year round.

Though we often picture them building bowl-shaped nests from sticks and twigs, birds actually build hundreds of different types of nests. Cavity nesters live in the trunks of trees, either in natural hollows or holes they peck themselves. Ravens nest high on cliff faces in cracks or crevices. While the nest itself may be tucked out of sight, its location can be picked out by "whitewash" below the nest, where the rock has been coated with bright white guano. The trumpeter swan, the largest bird native to North America, nests in a mound of floating vegetation. Osprey build nests of sticks, but favor a high vantage point typically over water. Look for their large nests atop the rock pinnacles that line the Grand Canyon of the Yellowstone.

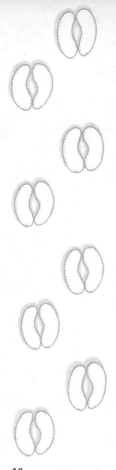

Some birds don't build nests at all, moving into abandoned nests or stealing nests from other birds. Cowbirds use a type of "parasitic nesting" because they migrate with the buffalo herds, never staying put long enough to nest. The cowbird cleverly lays her eggs in nests currently being used by other birds, leaving her eggs behind to blend in with the eggs of the nest builder. The surrogate parents will warm the eggs until they hatch, then feed and care for the young cowbirds as they care for their own chicks. Unfortunately, the cowbird quickly grows larger and more hungry than its adopted siblings, who may starve or get pushed out of the nest. Parasitic nesting ensures the cowbird's survival as a species, though scientists worry about the effects on the species who end up raising a cowbird and lose their own young.

Whatever type of nest they use, nesting season is a critical time for birds. Most birds will aggressively defend their nests from predators. If you are walking a Yellowstone trail and encounter a bird behaving strangely, consider that the bird may be protecting a nest. Circle generously around the area to avoid disturbing the nest. Observe warnings posted along roads and trails to avoid sensitive nesting habitats. Though humans do not pose the same threat to nesting birds as a hungry coyote might, our presence will distress the birds. Some species, such as the rare trumpeter swans, will fail to hatch their eggs if they encounter humans too closely during nesting.

Noodle Nests

6 cups chow mein noodles   ½ cup butter
4 ½ cups miniature marshmallows   45 small jelly beans

In a large saucepan over medium heat, melt the butter and marshmallows, stirring until smooth.

Add chow mein noodles and stir until noodles are coated with the marshmallow mixture.

With well-buttered hands, divide the noodles into nine sections. Rebuttering hands as needed, roll each section into a round ball.

Place each ball on a sheet of waxed paper coated with nonstick cooking spray. Using the back of a spoon, press each ball in the middle to form an indentation. Let the "nests" sit until they are firm.

Fill each nest with jelly beans before serving.

Where Are All The Bears?

There's an old joke in my family that whenever someone is looking for one of my teenage brothers they should check in front of the refrigerator. The grazing habitat of a teenage boy seems to extend in a rough circle between the fridge, pantry, table, and television. The habitats of Yellowstone wildlife are a bit more complex than my brother's, but the principle is the same: to find an animal, know what it eats. Finding food is a matter of life and death in the animal kingdom, and much of an animal's time is dedicated to doing just that.

In spite of this pressure to find food, many animals do not feel safe leisurely munching on their dinner in broad daylight, preferring to eat or hunt in the dark of night. This eating habit is characteristic of *nocturnal* animals. But many animals get hungry before it is truly dark, particularly during the long days of a Yellowstone summer, venturing out in the late evening to find something to eat. Animals that are most active at dawn and dusk are called *crepuscular*. The early morning and late evening, then, become the best times of day to see wildlife in Yellowstone. But where to look?

RAISING AN EAGLE FAMILY IN YELLOWSTONE

For many years a massive mound of sticks and mud has been sitting high in an old, dead tree overlooking the Madison River. Once an active eagle nest, the site was abandoned when the west entrance road was built nearby. The vacant nest drew the attention of many travelers on the road, but remained uninhabited. Then, a few years ago, a pair of bald eagles came to Yellowstone to keep house in the ancient nest. With a busy park road running between the nest and the river, the reoccupation of this nest came as a surprise. Still, the pair moved in and soon eaglets were on their way.

Eagles, who mate for life, start a new nest or find an abandoned nest, then spend many years adding more sticks and twigs to keep the nest strong. Two or three eggs are laid in late winter, and both the male and female birds incubate the eggs for the next thirty-four to thirty-six days. Initially, downy eaglets depend entirely on their parents for food, but after about three months they can begin to fly from the nest. While the sight of a bald eagle perched in a tree above the Madison River is enough to cause a traffic jam, the sight of young fledglings testing their wings can completely stop traffic along the west entrance road.

After two successful years of nesting along the Madison, the eagle pair had some bad luck. In spring 2004, the massive nest proved too heavy for the long-dead pine tree that had held it high above the river for so long. During strong winds the top of the tree snapped, dropping the nest several feet where it caught on a lower branch. The eaglets, unable to fly, fell hundreds of feet to the ground and died. Such nest instability is not uncommon in Yellowstone, where snags left from the 1988 fires are falling in greater numbers every year.

Initial studies of the nest suggest that the structure has been occupied for hundreds of years, providing a home to hundreds of eagles atop a tree overlooking the Madison River. When eagles were not around, other birds moved in. Some osprey made an attempt to use the nest with the prime fishing habitat, and a few geese successfully nested in the abandoned eagle's nest. For now it seems the Madison eagles are not quite ready to give up on their historic home. The summer after their nest fell, the eagles were observed carrying sticks and mud to patch up the gigantic nest. If their repairs are sufficient, we may once again see eaglets stretching their wings to take flight over the Madison River.

The elusive moose frustrates many Yellowstone visitors who see more moose in Grand Teton National Park than Yellowstone. The moose population is low in Yellowstone—fewer than 1,000 animals—due to the availability of food. Moose browse on woody vegetation, particularly willow, gooseberry, and buffalo berry, which take time to grow taller than the deep winter snow. A moose's summer diet is varied by aquatic plants like water lilies and duckweed, which gives a clue for finding

moose in Yellowstone. Look for marshy areas, willow flats, and shores of lakes and rivers, particularly those surrounded by thick forest where moose can rest during the heat of the day.

The other Yellowstone ungulates—hoofed mammals including elk, deer, and bison—are easier to find because they don't mind eating right out in the open. They graze on grasses, sedges, and shrubs found in meadows throughout the park. By running their food through several distinct stomach compartments these animals can draw much more nourishment from grass than a human stomach would be able to. When snow covers those grasses in the winter, the ungulates still must find food. Elk and deer migrate to lower elevations outside the park to find easier forage. Only the Madison Firehole elk herd stays in Yellowstone year-round, perhaps because the heat of the thermal features in their territory keeps snow levels down. After they dig through snow to nibble on dried grasses all winter, imagine the treat of finding green grass growing in a geyser basin in the middle of January!

While the ungulates are busy searching for their food, other animals are sizing them up for dinner. Where the elk are, the wolves will be also (along with the bears, coyotes, ravens, eagles, magpies, and any other animals who feed on the carcasses after the wolves open them). Since wolves were restored to Yellowstone in 1995, searching for these canines has become a popular activity, particularly in the Lamar Valley, home of the famous Druid Peak pack. In this observation we have seen how wolves feed the entire ecosystem. Ravens follow wolf packs as they go out to hunt, hoping to swoop in on a free meal if the hunt is successful. Once the animal is down, the wolves are kept busy eating the best parts of the carcass and chasing off coyotes hoping to snatch a bite or two. If the wolves don't defend their leftovers, other animals will move in, digesting every edible part of the carcass and recycling all those nutrients back into the energy system.

One animal, however, is often too impatient to take turns; bears are notorious for chasing wolves away from their hard-earned dinner. While bears can very well kill their own dinner, they seem to find it easier to steal someone else's. Bears will plant themselves on a carcass for days if they feel so inclined. Though we often visualize bears chewing on a carcass, bears, like us, need to eat their vegetables—and lots of them. They must build up an eight-inch layer of fat to survive the winter, so they dedicate most of their summertime to eating. When bears seem to wander aimlessly through meadows, they actually are searching deliberately for food. They turn over buffalo chips, licking insects off the bottom. They dig for roots. And they follow their keen sense of smell to fresh carcasses in the distance.

The variety in bears' diets takes them all over the park. Noticing a few trends may help you narrow your search for Yellowstone's star animal. When the bear emerges from hibernation in late winter, fresh food is still scarce, so they may turn to frozen dinners. Animals who perish in the winter often lie frozen until the spring thaw carries their smell to hungry bears. In spring, when the ground is still frozen, animal herds congregate in the less snowy valleys, so the bears go there to find food. Elk calves are a favorite bear food, so look for bears in the meadows where elk might graze. As summer progresses, food becomes a little scarcer and the need for calories becomes more urgent. Bears move to higher elevations to find swarms of cutworm moths and to eat the rich and fatty nuts of the white-bark pine tree, which grows above 7,000 feet in elevation. Bears hibernate in the winter because they cannot eat the dry vegetation that sustains ungulates

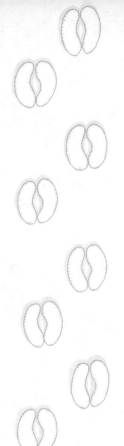

at this time of year. They survive the winter on the fat layer they built up during a busy summer of eating. Your chances of seeing bears in the winter are very slim: they don't need to eat, so they can spend those months tucked away in their dens.

YELLOWSTONE FISH FRY

At the height of summer look twice when you see that dark figure wading in the river; this time of year you are far more likely to see people standing knee deep in the river than water-loving wildlife like moose. When fishing season opens mid-June, hundreds of locals and visitors grab their poles and wade into the rivers for some of the best fishing around. They are up against tough competition, though, for dozens of winged and four-legged anglers are also scoping the waters for dinner. Bears, otters, mink, ospreys, pelicans, and bald eagles are among the many animals who feast on Yellowstone's fantastic fish.

Almost half of the water in Yellowstone was barren of fish when the park was established. The Firehole River had no fish above the Firehole Falls, and Shoshone and Lewis lakes were both fishless. In response to the popularity of angling, these areas were stocked with fish early in the park's history, introducing nonnative fish and dramatically altering the status of the eleven native fish species. Though the populations of native fish are still threatened (see box on page 56), fisheries managers in the park work to preserve both the fish and their habitats as well as the opportunity for anglers to catch wild fish in their beautiful, natural setting.

Today, the native fish most likely to be snagged by anglers are cutthroat trout, mountain whitefish, and arctic grayling. Other introduced trout species (rainbow, brown, brook, and lake) can still be found in Yellowstone's waters, and these species can usually be taken back to camp for a tasty dinner. *See park fishing regulations for limits and locations on non-native species. All native species are catch and release. To prevent lead poisoning in waterfowl, all tackle must be lead-free. Fishing permits are required, available for purchase at visitor centers throughout the park.*

Fish in Foil

1 trout, cleaned, head removed
1 clove garlic, sliced
1 lemon, sliced
1 small onion, sliced

1 small tomato, sliced
Fresh basil
Fresh rosemary
Salt and pepper

Prepare grill over campfire or burn fire until hot coals begin to form.

Stuff the fish cavity with prepared ingredients, adjusting seasonings to taste.

Wrap the fish in foil and set on grill or nestle into coals.

Cook 15–20 minutes, turning once. Turn back tin foil and use a fork to check fish. When fish flakes easily, remove from heat. Spoon out filling onto plate, discarding lemon slices.

Scrape the meat from the bones with a fork, combing out small bones.

Serve fish with the filling on the side and fresh lemon wedges.

WHERE THE BUFFALO ROAM

Today, more than 4,000 bison roam wild Yellowstone. As you drive by wide herds of buffalo (and get stuck in a two-hour traffic jam in Hayden Valley because bison are wandering down the road), it

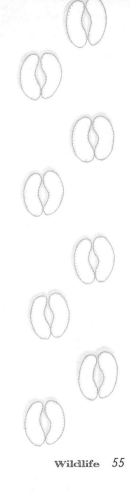

A FISHY INVASION

On July 29, 1994, a young girl fishing caught the first identified lake trout from the waters of Yellowstone Lake. These large, deep-dwelling fish threaten the population of native cutthroat trout, a much smaller fish. Not only do the larger trout eat the cutthroat, but they also take over vital spawning grounds and compete for food sources.

The impact of the lake trout on the cutthroat extends to other animals as well. Cutthroat trout are a primary source of food for animals that live on and around Yellowstone Lake. Pelicans and osprey feed on the fish, and when the fish are spawning grizzly bears line up along the creeks in hopes of catching dinner. Lake trout, who usually swim in the deep lake waters, are inaccessible to birds that fish in shallow waters. The decline in cutthroat populations means fewer fish are near the surface and dinner will be a lot harder for that pelican to come by. Lake trout are unable to replace cutthroat trout in the food chain.

In the last decade thousands of nonnative lake trout have been fished from Yellowstone Lake. In spite of removing 56,000 lake trout since 1995, scientists don't expect they will ever be able to eliminate this invasive species from Yellowstone's waters.

seems impossible that just one century ago, there were less than two dozen wild bison left in the lower forty-eight states. Those few animals lived in Yellowstone National Park, and their amazing comeback is one of the success stories of the National Park system. In the late 1800s, 60 million bison on the Great Plains were wiped out so rapidly that they were near extinction before anyone realized what was happening. Even in Yellowstone, bison were hunted and slaughtered for sport and game. When poaching regulations were at last enforced, only a handful of bison remained.

In 1906 and 1907, the military built the Buffalo Ranch in the Lamar Valley of Yellowstone. About twenty animals were purchased from domestic bison herds, and the attempt to restore the bison herd began. By the 1930s, the herd had grown to almost 1,000 animals. Initially a cause for celebration, the rising numbers also drew controversy. Today the management of Yellowstone's bison herd captures national attention every year. The natural instinct of the animals to wander out of the park in the hard winter season conflicts with wildlife and ranching concerns in bordering states.

Visitation numbers have risen in Yellowstone along with the size of the bison population, creating another cause for concern. More people in Yellowstone are injured by bison than by any other wild animals. People approach these animals like domestic cattle, without acknowledging their wild, unpredictable nature. *Always maintain at least twenty-five yards between you and a bison.* Visitors who have been gored by bison often receive a double punishment: the puncture wound from the bison horn, and a fine for approaching wildlife.

No one knows the wild nature of bison better than those who try to raise them domestically. Bison farms have become more abundant in recent years, as this lean alternative to beef grows in popularity. If you can't find bison for your stew at your local market, you can even order the meat online!

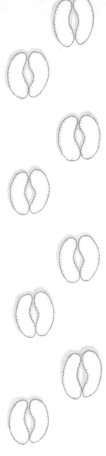

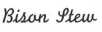

Bison Stew

1 ½ pounds boneless bison round steak
1 teaspoon vegetable oil
½ teaspoon dried whole thyme
2 large cloves garlic, minced
1 ½ cups apple juice
1 ½ cups red grape juice or cooking wine
¼ cup tomato paste
2 bay leaves
2 (13 and ¾ ounce) cans beef broth
½ cup water

1 ½ pounds red potatoes, quartered
½ pound fresh mushrooms, quartered
6 medium carrots, peeled and cut into
   1-inch pieces
2 small onions, sliced
3 tablespoons cornstarch dissolved in
   ¼ cup water
¼ cup chopped fresh parsley
½ teaspoon salt
¼ teaspoon pepper

Coat a large Dutch oven with cooking spray. Pour vegetable oil into preheated Dutch oven.

Cut bison steak into 1-inch cubes. Brown in oil.

Add the rest of the ingredients and stir. Situate Dutch oven over hot coals, placing a few on the lid for even heating.

Cook until meat and vegetables are tender, about four hours.

Note: If you're eatin' in the comfort of your own home, you can cook your bison stew in a crock pot. Brown meat on a skillet, then throw all ingredients into the crock pot. Cook on low 6–8 hours.

FARMING BISON

Early European settlers thought wild bison would be impossible to domesticate. Today, many ranchers who raise so-called domestic bison would likely agree. They might point to downed fences on their property or scars on their body to show that while they own a herd of bison, the animals carry a streak of wildness. As ranchers say, you can herd a bison just about anywhere it wants to go.

Bison meat, however, is becoming increasingly popular, now seen frequently in supermarkets. The meat tastes somewhat like beef, though that streak of wildness also seems to bring out a hint of "gamey" flavor. The meat is lower in cholesterol and leaner than traditional beef, making it a healthy choice for your dinner table.

A Fed Bear Is a Dead Bear

Many visitors to Yellowstone remember seeing dozens of bears along the roads in the park. Roadside bear feeding was a common practice during much of the twentieth century. With stomachs not too different from our own, bears could consume hundreds of marshmallows and crackers offered from car windows. As we all know, candy bars are a great way to build up fat, and bears found begging for food was an easy way to develop the fat needed for hibernation. Some visitors continue to mourn the management decisions of the 1960s and 1970s that forced bears back to natural food sources.

Today, instead of handing out food to bears, visitors to bear country actively try to keep food out of the reach of bears. Bear-proof garbage cans keep bears from digging through food scraps and other waste. Yellowstone campers are required to store food and food containers in their vehicles where odors can't reach bears' noses. (Bears in Yellowstone have not yet learned to recognize food by sight, so this park does not have the same problem as parks in northern California. There, bears will force their way into a vehicle when a cooler is visible.) The National Park Service and nearby towns closed open-pit garbage dumps and established laws to ensure that bears do not have easy access to human food.

Notable consequences resulted from these bear management policies. Bears have indeed returned to natural sources for their food. Not only are bears healthier feeding on roots and berries, but humans are healthier as well, for while we fed bears, they, literally, bit the hands that fed them. Imagine feeding a bear out your car window. His paws are propped up on the window sill and he bobs his head around as you tuck marshmallows into his mouth. But what happens if the bear wants ten or twelve marshmallows and you have only six or seven? Where's that bear going to look for more when you run out? And is there really room for you, the driver, and a 400-pound grizzly bear in the front seat? During the years that bears were being fed along roads and in the park dumps, there were, on average, forty-eight injuries to humans each year in Yellowstone. Since the bears have gone back to eating natural grub, that number has dropped dramatically. Now the park averages less than one bear-inflicted injury per year.

The bear management plan also aroused concern that the bear population would decline because bears had learned to depend on human food sources. Counting bears is a difficult task, but the best estimates suggest that after forty years of closed dumps the bear population is doing just fine. As long as bears continue to follow their natural diet, their odds of survival increase as well. As the popular motto says, "a fed bear is a dead bear." Bears have an exceptionally good memory when it comes to food, a skill they need in order to remember from year to year when the berries are ripe and where. So if they find food in a campground, they won't likely forget about it—and they'll be back. Unlucky for you if the people who stayed in your site last night left a loaf of bread out. If bears continue to come into a campground or picnic area for food, the odds of human injury rise. Eventually the bear will be relocated, but if she comes back—and bears have been known to travel hundreds of miles in order to return to a home territory—she may have to be exterminated. How much better things would have been if she had never been fed in the first place!

Yellowstone is a smorgasbord for bears, with all the strawberries and elk calves they can eat. It seems the population will be just fine if we leave them wild. While we may not see as many bears while driving through Yellowstone, few visitors forget the experience of seeing a sow grizzly meandering through a meadow, teaching her cubs how to find food in the Yellowstone wilderness.

Yellow-Beary Frozen Sorbet

If everyone follows the established rules in Yellowstone, bears aren't likely to be seen licking on an ice-cream cone. Knowing how bears love berries, however, we are confident they'd enjoy some Yellow-Beary Sorbet on a hot summer's day. While the bears are busying harvesting the summer berry crop, mix up some sorbet and join in on the berry feast!

Use your favorite berries to flavor this frozen treat. If you don't have an ice cream freezer, try using plastic bags to freeze your sorbet, as described below. But don't forget to put on some winter gloves!

Yellow-Beary Frozen Sorbet

1 cup sugar

1 cup water

4 cups berries, fresh or frozen

4 medium apples

¼ cup orange juice

Dissolve sugar in water in a small saucepan. Cook over medium heat just until mixture comes to a boil. Remove from stove and chill in the refrigerator.

Peel, core, and chop apples into large chunks. In a food processor or blender, puree the berries and apples. Strain out seeds if necessary. Add orange juice and blend.

Pour berries and syrup into an ice cream freezer and mix well. Freeze according to instructions on freezer.

If you are making sorbet in the wild, bring along a small box of rock salt, large and small sealable plastic bags (sandwich size and freezer size), ice cubes, and a couple pairs of winter gloves. You can make the sorbet mix at home, then chill in your cooler until ready to freeze. Pour about 1 ½ cups sorbet mix into a sandwich bag. Seal tightly. Fill the bottom of a freezer bag with ice cubes and a few tablespoons of rock salt. Set sandwich bag inside freezer bag on top of ice. Add more ice and rock salt until freezer bag is about half full. Seal freezer bag.

FOOD FOR THOUGHT . . .

Bears aren't the only animal in Yellowstone clever enough to realize that the two-legged creatures that migrate into the park each year bring along lots of tasty things to eat. Picnickers in the park may feel rushed through their meal by Clark's nutcrackers and Stellar jays lying wait in the trees for their chance at the table scraps. Folks waiting for Old Faithful may notice yellow-bellied marmots scampering under the boardwalks looking for the potato chip that fell out of someone's lunch or a melting scoop of ice cream that slid off the cone. Clever ravens have even learned to unzip the food compartments on the backs of snowmobiles that come into the park in the winter. Finding food is essential for animals to survive, and humans who carry their food with them are an easy target. Resist the urge to feed them, though. If they don't know how to feed themselves on natural foods, they don't stand a chance of survival during those long months when humans aren't around.

With gloved hands, toss the plastic bags from hand to hand, agitating the mixture inside. Continue working the bag until sorbet begins to firm. This could take several minutes, so keep those gloves on! When sorbet Is frozen and set, remove sandwich bag from freezer bag and *rinse well*. (This prevents the salty water from leaking into your sorbet.) Open sandwich bag and turn out contents into a bowl—or eat it right from the bag.

BEARS AND BERRIES

Bears are creative and enthusiastic eaters—they have to be in order to consume the thousands of calories they need each day to prepare for the winter. Because they're in such a hurry, they don't have a lot of time for delicately picking berries, a fruit they very much love to eat. Instead, they often clamp their mouths over a branch and strip it clean, berries, leaves and all.

Bears' affinity for berries works to the plant's advantage. Many seeds from the berries pass through the animal's digestive system intact. When the bear poops, these seeds return to the ground packed with fertilizer and ready to start a new berry community. During the summer berry season, bear scat differs from other carnivores because it often contains more berries than hair.

Bears have an excellent memory when it comes to food. As they circulate around their home ranges, they learn just where the berry patches are and what time of year the berries ripen. They return to the same patches year after year to indulge in a sweet treat just when the berries are coming into season.

Chapter Three
Plants

Most of the species of mushrooms found in Yellowstone National Park are poisonous—which means the odds aren't in your favor if you pick a wild 'shroom for your stew. People have died in Yellowstone because they ate the wrong plant. Fortunately, most people don't come to Yellowstone to eat plants, but to look at their displays of color and sculpture. On a drive or hike through Yellowstone, particularly during the spring and early summer, you will enjoy a show of vegetation unlike any other in the world. With its acidic soils and long winters, the Yellowstone plateau is a tough climate for plants to take root and grow, and yet the park is home to hundreds of wildflowers, eight types of coniferous trees, and several rare plants that can only be found in the hydrothermal areas.

Humans have had a dramatic influence on the plantscape of Yellowstone. The introduction of exotic species, which threaten to take over the soil by strangling out native plants, is a constant concern for botanists in Yellowstone. Even picking individual plants can have far-reaching effects, particularly in areas like geyser basins that are both highly fragile and highly visited. In order to protect native vegetation, regulations against picking plants in Yellowstone are strongly enforced, and picking even a single wildflower can result in a fine for resource damage. The one exception to this rule is picking berries, nuts, and mushrooms for *immediate, personal* consumption. You can't preserve them to take home with you, and you can't gather bushels to feed all your friends and family, but if you're walking a trail and see that wild strawberry—and have positively identified it as safe to eat—go ahead and grab it. You'd better grab quickly, though, because there is a great deal of competition for food in Yellowstone. Bears and other animals like many of the same foods we do, but they depend on these foods for calories to survive the winter. If you can find berries and mushrooms in your own garden or supermarket, consider using them in your cooking and leaving Yellowstone's plants for the wildlife to eat for dinner.

The following recipes will help you become familiar with the appearance, function, and flavor of plants that grow in the Yellowstone area. Many of the recipes are made with native plants. If you are cooking away from Yellowstone, are unsure about identifying the appropriate varieties of wild plants, or simply aren't up for the effort of gathering your own leafy greens, supermarket substitutions are provided. You may be surprised by the number of Yellowstone plants and berries you already serve at your table.

Parmesan Pinecone

Yellowstone is not an easy place to grow a tree. With snow on the ground almost eight months out of the year, the trees are basically living in a refrigerator—or a freezer. The topsoil comes from eroding rhyolite, which has both the texture and the nutritional value of ground glass. Even at its best, the soil is mildly acidic and less than a foot deep. Some areas receive less than ten inches of rainfall (mostly in the form of snow) per year. Not an easy place for a young tree to grow up. In fact, only eleven types of trees manage to grow in Yellowstone, eight of which are *conifers,* or cone-bearing trees.

All conifers have two types of cones—male and female. Male cones produce pollen, which fertilizes female cones. After pollination, the female cones develop and release the tree's seeds. Looking at a tree's cones can help you identify the type of tree. If the cones are growing upright on the tree, sitting on top of the branches, you may be looking at a *subalpine fir.* The *Douglas fir* tree has cones that hang down from the branches and have three-pronged bracts between the scales (many people are reminded of a furry mouse scampering into the cone with just its hind legs and tail poking out). The *Englemann spruce* also has hanging cones but no bracts in the cone. When you look at a *lodgepole, limber,* or *whitebark pine* tree, notice the male and female cones. The many stages of cone growth make it seem like four or five types of cones are growing on the same tree. The *Rocky Mountain juniper* and its shrublike cousin, the common juniper, have small, fleshy cones and berries.

Parmesan Pinecone

1 cup sliced almonds

12 ounces cream cheese, softened

½ cup grated parmesan cheese

¼ cup mayonnaise

2 teaspoons fresh oregano, chopped (½ teaspoon dried)

1 clove garlic, minced

½ cup sunflower seeds

Toast almonds in a skillet over medium-high heat, stirring frequently until almonds are evenly browned.

Combine cheeses, mayonnaise, oregano, and garlic. Refrigerate one hour.

When cheese mixture is firm enough, transfer to a serving platter. Work into the elongated shape of a pinecone. Using your palms, press sunflower seeds into surface of the cheese. Then arrange almonds around cheese mixture to simulate the growth of pine bracts.

Serve with crackers.

PINE NEEDLE PASTA

Most of us can't tell the difference between the tall pine trees we see in Yellowstone and that tree we drag into our living rooms each December—except perhaps that in Yellowstone they don't come with shiny glass globes and flashing lights. If you look a little closer, however, you'll begin to see some differences, and maybe some similarities, between the forests at Yellowstone and the trees in your own backyard.

To identify a Yellowstone conifer, start by looking at the needles. Do the needles come in bunches? Only the Yellowstone pine trees grow clusters of needles. In order to separate lodgepole from limber or whitebark, count the needles in a single cluster.

Are the needles in bunches of two? Or five? Lodgepole pines have needles in groups of two; limber and whitebark pine have groups of five. Remember, two needles form an *L* for lodgepole.

Do the needles grow individually? Spruce and fir tree needles grow singly. To tell them apart, try pulling a needle from the tree and rolling it between your thumb and finger.

FIERY CONES

As the female cone of the lodgepole pine matures, it releases seeds onto the forest floor. Because the forest is so thick with trees, sunlight barely reaches the ground to help the seedlings grow. Meanwhile, young shade-loving trees, like the subalpine or Douglas firs, grow up under the lodgepole canopy and attempt to take over the lodgepole forest.

Fortunately the lodgepole pine has a secret weapon waiting in the wings: forest fire. While some of the cones release their seeds upon maturity, others are sealed up with a waxy resin, holding onto the new seeds. These serotinous *cones may cling to the trees for years, waiting for the perfect opportunity to release the seeds. Forest fire provides just that opportunity. The heat from the fire melts the resin, scattering the seeds all over the forest floor. The fire burns the needles off the old trees, clearing the forest canopy, and allowing rays of sun to light up the forest floor. Now, with plenty of sunlight, the seedlings can grow into a healthy, new lodgepole forest.*

Many visitors marvel at the density of these young saplings, assuming that surely some have been replanted. Under good conditions and with a high percentage of serotinous-cone-bearing trees, the natural regrowth can be quite thick. In one area where half of the trees had serotinous cones, 1.9 million seedlings were counted in one hectare (2.5 acres) of ground.

Does it roll easily? Spruce needles are square in the cross-section, rolling easily between our fingers. If you can't roll the needle, that's probably because it is flat. If you snap a fir needle in half and look at the end, you can see its flat shape.

How do they feel? Lightly grab a handful of needles in your palm. If you flinch and pull away, you've probably grabbed a sharp spruce. If you can hold the needles easily in your palm, you're holding a blunt fir needle. Think "friendly fir, spiny spruce."

But there are two types of firs, and three types of pines . . . Now you have to look at the cones. Remember the "furry" mouse coming out of the Douglas fir cone? Check the forest floor for these cones, which fall easily from the tree. If you don't see them, you're probably standing under a subalpine fir tree.

Whitebark and limber pines both have needles in clusters of five, so again we look at the cones. Whitebark cones are small and oval-shaped; limber cones are much longer, stretching up to seven inches. You might also consider your elevation. Whitebark pine grows at higher elevations than limber pine. Thus limber pine is seen commonly on the Mammoth Hot Springs terraces, while whitebark pine grows on mountain peaks and in high areas on the east entrance road.

What about the juniper? Rocky Mountain juniper look different from all the other pine trees in Yellowstone, often growing low to the ground. Look for short, short needles growing singly on the branch. These scale-like needles are often bluish in color.

You can practice your conifer identification skills by making a dish of pine needle pasta. You'll break up bits of pasta into a blend of needles, then top it with a pine-nut sauce, and sprinkle on some freshly grated cheese to include the tiny juniper needles.

Pine Needle Pasta

Pasta:

1 serving tonnarelli pasta (use directions on package to measure a serving)

1 serving linguine pasta (may substitute fettuccine)

2 servings trennette pasta (may substitute spaghetti)

Water

Dash of salt

Fill a large saucepan with water, salt, and bring to a boil. While water is heating, prepare pine needle noodles.

Spruce: Tonnarelli is a narrow, square-shaped noodle. Break the long, thin strands into pieces, about one inch long. Englemann spruce needles are square, about an inch in length.

Fir: Linguine is a flat noodle, narrower than fettuccine. Break these strands into 1-inch pieces, about the length of a Douglas or subalpine fir needle.

Pine: Trennette pasta has a triangular cross-section, close to the not-quite-round needle shape of pine needles. If you can't find trennette, use common spaghetti. The shape is approximate, and, as the most common pasta, spaghetti is appropriate to represent the most common tree in Yellowstone.

Pour needle noodles into boiling water and boil about seven minutes, or until pasta is soft but not mushy. Pour into colander and rinse with cold water.

Serve pine needle pasta with pesto sauce and freshly grated parmesan cheese (to represent the tiny needles of the juniper tree).

Pesto Sauce

3 garlic cloves

2 cups fresh basil leaves

4 tablespoons pine nuts

Dash salt and pepper

½ cup extra virgin olive oil

½ cup freshly grated parmesan cheese

Wash and dry basil leaves, removing stems. Mince garlic in food processor. Add basil leaves, pine nuts, salt and pepper to the food processor and blend. With the processor running on slow speed, drizzle olive oil in through the feed tube. Scrape sides of food processor bowl with rubber spatula and blend again. Add parmesan cheese, blend, and scrape sides again. Add water (about a tablespoon) to thin sauce if necessary. Refrigerate until ready to use, up to three days. Pesto also freezes well.

Note: Traditional pesto sauces are blended by hand with a mortar and pestle. If you prefer to make by hand, work the first four ingredients into a paste, then pound in parmesan cheese. Pour in oil and whisk until smooth. You may also make pesto in a blender if you do not have a food processor.

LODGEPOLE PRETZEL LOGS

Tall, skinny-trunked pine trees cover the hills and mountains of Yellowstone with a thick forest of green. These lodgepole pine trees begin growing sometimes just inches apart, stretching toward the sky in search of a little extra sunshine. Lower branches wither and die, unable to reach the light through the shade of the pine canopy, giving the tree its notable pencil-like straightness.

Few other trees can survive in Yellowstone's shallow, acidic soil, so lodgepoles have free rein over about 80 percent of the park.

Native Americans used these tall, straight trunks to erect their tepees or "lodges," giving the tree the common name of lodgepole pine. The scientific name, *pinus contorta,* seems less appropriate, as the straight trunk is anything but contorted. The same species of tree growing on the Pacific coast twists itself into knot-like shapes in the face of strong ocean winds. A closer examination of the lodgepole trunk in Yellowstone reveals a slight twist in the trunk as it stretches skyward, the only hint of its relationship to its contorted coastal cousins. This twist strengthens the trunk, allowing the tree to grow tall and strong even in high Yellowstone winds.

During hot, dry summers, such as Yellowstone faced in 1988, the lodgepole pine is susceptible to forest fire. Fast-moving crown fires blaze through the tops of the trees, singeing the needles, but leaving much of the trunk intact. Without its needles, the tree dies, but the naked trunk remains standing. These "snags" can stand for many years after a fire, until their roots decay and a strong wind blows them down. Now the trunk will slowly decompose, returning its nutrients back to the soil and nourishing the young lodgepole forest growing below.

Forest fires occur every year in Yellowstone National Park, but no fires have caught the attention of the world like the Yellowstone fires of 1988. During that summer about one-third of the park (793,880 acres) burned in more than fifty separate fires. Twenty-five thousand people worked to prevent historic buildings from being swept up in the lodgepole blaze, which burned until snow fell in September. Many of the trunks and embers smoldered through the following winter, leaving behind a blackened forest that horrified many travelers the following year.

Driving along Yellowstone's winding roads, visitors marvel at the wall of lodgepole pine stretching tunnel-like before them. Many mourn the burned forest when they see the stripped snags memorializing the fires of the past. But the cycle of the lodgepole repeats itself, opening the way for a healthy young forest to extend its trunks to the sky.

Lodgepole Pretzel Logs

40 chewy caramel candies, unwrapped, or 8 ounces caramel

5 teaspoons water

8 ounces semisweet or milk chocolate, finely chopped

8 pretzel sticks, approximately 8 inches long and ½ inch in diameter

Cover a cookie sheet with waxed paper and lightly coat with nonstick cooking spray.

Melt caramels in a saucepan over low heat, stirring frequently. Add up to 5 teaspoons water, 1 at a time, until soft and smooth. (If desired, you may melt in a covered, microwave-safe dish. Heat in microwave at half power, thirty seconds at a time, stirring regularly, until liquefied.)

Dip pretzels into caramel mixture, one at a time, swirling until the stick is coated halfway up its length. Pull pretzel from mixture, allowing excess caramel to drip while holding over bowl a few seconds. Place on prepared cookie sheet and let cool until firm. Repeat with all pretzel sticks or until caramel is used up.

Melt chocolate slowly in a double boiler over low heat, stirring constantly. Do not overheat. (In a microwave, heat a few seconds at a time, medium power, stirring frequently.) Remove from heat.

YELLOWSTONE IN WINTER

In the heart of the winter season, several feet of snow cover the Yellowstone plateau. Grasses and sedges are dead, dry, and buried, inaccessible to all but the most persistent grazers. When food grows scarce, animals look up to the trees for nourishment. With their bottom teeth, they scrape away the dry, tasteless bark, seeking out the juicier cambium layer below. This chewy wood contains more nutrients for the animal. If just part of the tree is browsed, the tree will survive, bearing a scar for the rest of its life. If the pretzel forms the core of your Lodgepole Pretzel Logs and the chocolate forms the bark, what might be the chewy cambium? Try licking away the bark, bison-like, then chewing on the caramel cambium of your tree.

Quickly dip caramel-coated pretzel trunks into liquid chocolate until caramel is covered. Shake off excess chocolate and place on waxed paper. Allow to cool and harden at room temperature. Repeat until all pretzels are coated.

WHITEBARK COOKIE BARK

Whitebark pine trees grow in the high elevations of Yellowstone National Park. These tall pines weather the elements to survive on chilly mountaintops more than 7,000 feet above sea level. As whitebark pines mature, they produce protein-packed pinecones. The tree relies on animals to open the cones and release the seeds into the ground. The Clark's nutcracker sets to work cracking open the cones with a sharp beak and tucking the seeds away for winter storage. An industrious nutcracker can transplant 30,000 seeds in a single season. Eager squirrels also collect cones—or steal the seeds from nutcracker caches—and stash them away in their own middens, stockpiles of food to sustain the rodents through the winter. As summer draws on, hungry bears wander up to higher elevations in search of extra calories. Bears seek out the pine nuts to build up the fat reserves they need to make it through the winter. Instead of gathering the tiny nuts themselves, clever bears sniff out the squirrel middens. By raiding the cache of pine nuts, bears can consume thousands of calories in just minutes, leaving all the work of finding and harvesting the nuts to the birds . . . and the squirrels.

Bears rely on the whitebark pine trees to provide food when the summer heat has withered vegetation at lower elevations. Threats to the whitebark pines also threaten the bear population. One of those threats comes in the form of a tiny insect called the mountain pine beetle (*Dendroctonus ponderosae*). Pine beetles burrow into the bark of trees to lay eggs and feast on the nutrient-rich layers underneath. The tree may be able to purge the beetle from its bark by targeting the infestation with oozing sap, but often the tree is unable to resist the parasite, and the insects take over, eventually killing the tree.

Pine beetles spend almost their entire lives under the bark of the tree, emerging for just one day in adulthood to find a new host tree. In those few hours, the beetle can travel more than a dozen miles in search of a new home. When it finds a healthy pine, it burrows into the bark where it mates, lays eggs, and begins the cycle again.

Brown, dry forests in Yellowstone and around the western United States testify to the power of a miniscule insect to enact dramatic change upon a landscape. Dead pine trees stand where green forests once grew, awaiting the tiny spark that will set the mountain ablaze. The 1988 fires in Yellowstone eradicated much of the pine beetle population in the lodgepole forests that cover the park. The whitebark pine, spared to some extent from the fires, continue to suffer the pine beetle invasion. As more and more trees die, researchers are beginning to wonder whether the declining whitebark population will impact other creatures, like Clark's nutcrackers, squirrels, and grizzly bears. They must examine the purpose of this tiny, yet powerful, pine beetle in the Yellowstone ecosystem.

Whitebark Cookie Bark

1 package (20 ounces) creme-filled chocolate sandwich cookies
1 package (18 ounces) white chocolate, bars, chunk, or chips
1 package (18 ounces) milk or semisweet chocolate

Prepare a jellyroll pan (10 x 15 inch) with waxed paper. Spray with nonstick cooking spray.

Pour cookies into a large, resealable plastic bag. Use fingers or a rolling pin to break cookies into coarse pieces (not crumbs).

Melt white chocolate in a microwave-safe bowl, 30 seconds at a time on low power. Stir frequently until melted. Remove from microwave and pour half of the cookie pieces into melted chocolate. Stir until coated. Spoon mixture onto prepared pan, spreading but not covering the entire pan. Scrape bowl well using rubber spatula.

Melt dark chocolate in microwave in the same manner. Add remaining cookie pieces and stir until coated. Spoon mixture onto jellyroll pan, filling in holes in the white chocolate. Cut spatula through the two kinds of chocolate to create marbled effect.

Refrigerate until set, at least one hour.

Turn pan onto cutting board or sheet of waxed paper. Carefully peel the waxed paper off the cookie bark. Cut into chunks with large knife or break with fingers.

WILD STRAWBERRY SMOOTHIES

A good, wet spring in Yellowstone brings a lush berry season. Berries are a favorite sweet treat for bears and other animals, including humans. If you hike at just the right time of year, you may see wild berries along many of Yellowstone's trails. In late June and July, you can watch the white flowers of wild strawberry plants turn to sweet red berries. The needles of a raspberry bush may prick you as you descend down the steep banks of a river. You may also stumble on berries at Yellowstone that you aren't used to seeing in grocery stores at home, such as the grouse whortleberry, a tiny purple berry growing on low bushes that blanket the forest floor. Wild berries tend to be smaller than the varieties we buy from the supermarket, but they are often sweeter and tastier. If you are cooking in Yellowstone, see if you can find some berries to sweeten up these recipes. If you are at home, go ahead and use berries bought at the grocery store. The bears will gladly eat all the berries we leave them.

It will take a lot of wild strawberries to make these smoothies, as wild varieties of this common berry don't grow much bigger than a pea. Buying berries from a fruit stand or market will save you lots of picking time, or you can use frozen berries from your grocery store.

Strawberry Smoothie

1 cup milk

2 cups fresh strawberries, diced
(may substitute frozen berries,
adding additional berries to taste)

⅓ cup sugar

½ teaspoon vanilla

Combine ingredients in blender. Add 12–14 ice cubes, a few at a time, until smooth and frothy. Pour into glasses and serve cold.

HUCKLEBERRY PANCAKES

Many people consider the huckleberry to be the best-tasting berry in Yellowstone. A visit to one of the general stores confirms that humans have a passion for this deep-purple berry. Shoppers can load their souvenir bags with everything from huckleberry chocolate and ice cream to huckleberry hand cream and scented soaps.

Huckleberries grow abundantly in the wild in Yellowstone and surrounding areas. The fruit resembles blueberries in size and shape, though the texture is a little crunchier. Huckleberry plants have not been cultivated for commercial production, so the berries remains a wild, spontaneous

treat for the lucky hiker who stumbles upon a patch. Beginning in August, look for ripe berries on low shrubs in the lodgepole forests in the southern part of the Yellowstone region. If you find a full bush, you can quickly harvest a few by spreading a cloth below the plant and gently shaking the ripe berries loose. Gather up your cloth and head back to camp for some Huckleberry Pancakes.

If you can't find huckleberry plants at home—or if a bear beat you to them—go ahead and toss in fresh or frozen blueberries for a nearly huckleberry flavor.

Huckleberry Pancakes

1 egg, beaten

1 cup flour

1 cup buttermilk

1 tablespoon sugar

2 tablespoons butter or margarine, melted

½ teaspoon baking powder

½ teaspoon baking soda

½ teaspoon salt

1 teaspoon lemon juice

1 teaspoon vanilla

1 to 1 ½ cups berries, to taste

Sift flour, sugar, powder, soda, salt into a mixing bowl. Melt butter or margarine in a large measuring cup. Add egg and buttermilk. Mix until blended. Add wet to dry, mix, then add lemon juice and vanilla. Mix well, though batter will have lumps. Add fresh berries to batter just before cooking, or drop individual berries into pancakes after pouring on the griddle. (If using frozen berries, thaw, rinse, and drain berries before adding to batter.)

With a small measuring cup, ladle a scant ¼ cup of batter onto a preheated, greased griddle or skillet. Cook over medium-high heat until bubbles appear and solidify around edges of pancake. When lightly browned on one side, carefully flip and cook on opposite side until cooked through. Serve with warm maple or huckleberry syrup.

Rose Hip Jam

As the berry season passes and winter settles onto the Yellowstone plateau, much of the vegetation fades into winter dormancy. One common Yellowstone shrub, the wild rose *(rosa woodsii)*, drops its bright pink petals, but the valuable fruits, called rose hips, remain on the branches through the winter. These berry-like hips, identified by their hairy tails, are available to animals long after most other fruits have withered. The hips that last the winter provide nutrients for early-rising bears who emerge from hibernation while snow still covers the ground. These fruits are an excellent source of vitamins, including vitamins A, B, C, E, and K. You may also find rose hips in the manufactured vitamins in your cabinet, particularly in capsules of vitamin C.

You can gather rose hips from wild and domestic rose bushes to use in cooking. The moderately sweet fruit is best harvested just after the first frost, after the bloom has died. Collect hips that are slightly soft but not withered or squishy. Pluck off the hairy tails, wash the hips, then spread them out to dry. When the skin is slightly wrinkled, pop open the hips to remove the seeds. These seeds are covered with tiny hairs that can irritate the digestive system, causing "itchy bottom disease" on their way out. Finish drying the hips for munching on later, or use them to make Rose Hip Jam.

Rose Hip Jam

2 pounds rose hips

4 green apples

2 ½ pounds granulated sugar

⅓ cup lemon juice

6 cups water

Cut rose hips in halves lengthwise, removing spines and "tails." Heat 4 cups of water to a boil and add rose hips. Boil about fifteen minutes, until tender. Pour into a fine sieve. Mash hips through sieve to separate seeds. Discard seeds.

Peel and core apples. Boil apples in 2 cups water, cooking until soft. Press apples through a sieve to puree, or blend in a food processor.

Combine rose hips and apple puree in a large saucepan. Add sugar and lemon juice and bring to a boil. Boil 15 minutes, stirring frequently.

Pour jam into small, sterile jars. Use immediately, freeze, or seal jars tightly with canning lids.

PEPPERY PRICKLY PEAR SALAD

When folks in Yellowstone ask, "Is it going to rain today?" the sarcastic, one-word answer "Somewhere" is not too far from the truth. During the summer, afternoon thunderstorms are common. But while it rains at Old Faithful, skies may be blue over the rest of the park.

The amount of annual rainfall varies considerably around Yellowstone. The Bechler region gets drenched with an average of eighty inches per year, while the northern area around Mammoth Hot Springs parches with less than ten inches annually. With so little moisture, areas in the north look more like a desert than a mountain forest. Here the vegetation turns to sage-brush flats, and if you peer down between the sage plants you are likely to find small prickly pear cacti. Yellowstone prickly pear don't grow very big, but their colorful blooms, in shades of red, yellow, and peach, radiate color in the desert landscape.

To prepare prickly pear for eating, you have to first get rid of those pesky spines. You can break off the larger needles with a gloved hand, then burn off the rest with a blowtorch or by holding the cactus paddle over the stove. Then peel off the tough outer layer using a knife. The inner flesh is juicy and edible, and can now be cut into chunks like any other vegetable. If prickly pears don't grow in your area, look for canned cactus in the exotic foods section of your grocery store.

Peppery Prickly Pear Salad

3 cans cactus or
   6 cups fresh prickly pear
2 fresh tomatoes
1 can tomatoes

1 can green chilies
3 jalapenos
1 fresh lime, or 3 tablespoons lime juice
Fresh cilantro

Dressing:
  ½ cup mayonnaise
  2 tablespoons red wine vinegar
  1 tablespoon lime juice
  2 tablespoons vegetable oil
  1 tablespoon water

1 teaspoon soy sauce
½ teaspoon dried oregano
1 teaspoon sugar
1 teaspoon pepper
1 clove garlic, crushed

Dash chili powder (to taste)

Drain cans of cactus and rinse thoroughly, removing stems. Mix all ingredients for dressing in mixing bowl or salad dressing shaker.

Pour dressing over drained cactus and marinate well.

Thinly slice the tomatoes, mince jalapenos, and drain the cans of tomatoes and chilies. Add these ingredients to the cactus and toss together.

Squeeze lime juice over the salad and mix in. Garnish with tomato slices and fresh cilantro. Chill before serving.

MORE MUSHROOMS, PLEASE

The wetter areas of Yellowstone have very different types of vegetation, even a few mushrooms here and there. Morel mushrooms *(Morchella angusticeps)* have a delicate flavor that is particularly tasty during rainy years. They can be found in the cool forests of Yellowstone during a few weeks of summer. Look for them along the trail, but as with all mushrooms, be certain you have a positive identification before sampling. Remember, when in doubt . . . throw it out! (You can always pick up some morels and onions for this sauce in your grocery store.)

Morel and Wild Onion Sauce

½ cup wild onions
1 cup morel mushrooms

½ teaspoon salt
2 teaspoons cornstarch

2 tablespoons olive oil   1 cup water
1 teaspoon sugar

Gather a handful of wild onions and two handfuls of morel mushrooms. Rinse well. Halve the mushrooms and slice the onions.

Dust onions with sugar. Heat olive oil on medium skillet. Sauté onions.

As the onions begin to brown and caramelize, add the morels to the skillet. Add the salt.

Simmer ten more minutes, adding a bit of water as needed to prevent sticking.

Dissolve 2 teaspoons cornstarch in 1 cup water. Add to skillet, gradually, just enough to make a thin sauce. Simmer a moment more and add more cornstarch/water mixture if needed. Simmer until desired consistency.

Serve over grilled steak, steamed vegetables, or noodles.

SHEEPEATER STEW

Could you make dinner using only ingredients that grow in Yellowstone National Park? With all the plants found in Yellowstone, that may not seem like a challenging task, but you may find it harder than it seems at first glance. The growing season is too short for most grains, so you can't use wheat or oats or corn in your recipe. You can't milk a bison, so dairy products are out. Most fruit-producing trees can't survive in the park's acidic soils. Potatoes grow well in that type of soil, but they aren't native to the park. Still, many people have managed to sustain themselves quite well on food found in the park, particularly the group of Shoshone Indians who called Yellowstone

home year-round. These people were known as the Sheepeaters because they hunted, among other game, bighorn sheep. Try out the recipe for Sheepeater Stew, seasoned only with items that can be found here in Yellowstone. Perhaps it wouldn't be so bad living off the land here after all.

Sheepeater Stew

2 pounds boneless lamb	2 cups chopped turnips
½ teaspoon salt	1 cup chopped carrots
2 tablespoons grease (vegetable oil)	2 ounces dried mushrooms
2 cups water	Handful dried sage leaves, crushed
2 onions, thinly sliced	

Rehydrate mushrooms in ½ cup hot water while preparing the lamb.

Rub lamb with salt. Cut into 1-inch cubes. Heat oil over medium high heat in a skillet or a 3-quart Dutch oven. Brown lamb in hot oil, a few pieces at a time. Remove lamb chunks from skillet and set aside on a serving platter or in a crock pot.

When all of the lamb has been browned, throw onion slices onto the skillet/Dutch oven and cook until browned, about three minutes. Add water to skillet, standing back to avoid splattering oil, and stir well, scraping bits of fried onion off the bottom of the pan.

Slice rehydrated mushrooms. Add to the onion mixture.

If using a crock pot, pour onion mixture into the crock pot. Add carrots and turnips to the meat and onions. Toss in seasoning. Cover and simmer on low for 8–10 hours.

In a Dutch oven, return meat to the onion mixture, then add carrots, turnips, and seasoning. Arrange coals on Dutch oven (to about 300 degrees) and cook, rotating frequently, 3–4 hours. Serves four.

How would you have cooked your stew in Yellowstone two centuries ago? You wouldn't have a crock pot to slowly simmer the meat and vegetables, and you might not have had a cast-iron Dutch oven either. Kettles and cookware acquired from European settlers through trade forever changed the Native American kitchen. So don't hesitate to use your new kitchen technology and cook your Sheepeater Stew in a crock pot.

The Sheepeaters dried and ground the roots of some plants to make flour for baking. The biscuitroot plant gets its name because it was used for this purpose. You probably won't find biscuitroot flour in your grocery store, but it wouldn't be too much of a compromise to serve your stew with Biscuit Basin Biscuits (page 20).

Thirty-Seven Days of Thistle

Most of us have felt, at some point in our lives, the terror of being lost. Whether we were separated from our mother at the department store and found sobbing in sporting goods on aisle 5, or found ourselves driving in circles through a strange city wondering just how we ended up in this dark corner of town, we have all felt the combination of despair and adrenaline that comes with being completely alone and out of place. Some have even experienced the life-shaking fear of

FATAL ROOTS

Because few visitors graze on Yellowstone's plants, death due to poisoning is rare in the park. One of the most tragic instances occurred deep in the interior of the park in April 1927. The Old Faithful innkeepers, a couple by the name of Bauer, found some plants growing along a warm stream. They brought them to the winter ranger, Charles Phillips, for identification. After deciding the plant was wild parsnip and would make a tasty variation on their winter fare of canned and dried goods, they prepared and ate the roots. After their eight o'clock dinner, Phillips returned to his cabin, and the innkeepers retired to bed. The Bauers awoke in the middle of the night, weak and vomiting. They remained indoors the next day, too violently ill to venture into the Yellowstone winter. When Mr. Bauer finally checked on Phillips, he found the ranger's cabin dark and cold, and Phillips lying, dead, on the kitchen floor. The plant, it turned out, was Water Hemlock, a deadly member of the parsnip family.

being lost in the wilderness, when disorientation mixes with worry over whether you will be able to find something to eat, and avoid being eaten yourself. Perhaps no one has experienced the distress of being lost to the extent that one early Yellowstone traveler did.

Truman Everts came to Yellowstone in 1870, a member of the Washburn-Langford-Doane expedition. This group of explorers came to the Yellowstone area to confirm rumors about a place where hot water boiled straight out of the ground and magnificent herds of wild animals roamed through forests of petrified trees. Everts, a fifty-four-year-old tax collector from Montana, decided to join the group in a final western adventure before moving to the East. In the next few weeks he would find more adventure than he could have possibly imagined.

On September 8, 1870, Everts became separated from the rest of the group as they were traveling through a maze of fallen lodgepole logs covering the ground around the south arm of Lake Yellowstone. At first, Everts felt little concern at his separation, confident that he would soon catch up with the rest of the group. When he didn't find them by nightfall, he unloaded his horse, cooked some dinner, and laid out his bedroll for the night, confident he would find them the next morning. When he awoke, Everts broke camp, reloaded his horse, and set out to find the group. The morning's search, however, revealed no sign of his traveling companions, and he grew more concerned. He climbed a ridge in hopes of seeing some sign of the group. Nothing spotted, he returned to the small meadow where he had left his horse, only to find the animal had run off. Now Everts was not only left without transportation, but he also lost all his supplies: no bedroll for sleeping, no maps for directions, no gear for fishing, no gun for hunting, and no pans for cooking. He had only the clothes he was wearing, the knife on his belt, and a pair of opera glasses hung 'round his neck.

When it began to snow four days into the ordeal, Everts knew he was in trouble. Fortunately he stumbled on the Heart Lake geyser basin and found a spot between two hot springs where he could keep warm whatever direction the wind was blowing. Now his thoughts turned to food. He had eaten nothing since that first night alone in the woods, and he was aching for strength and nourishment. Desperate for food, Everts turned to what was probably the biggest plant he could see: a tall thistle with a hardy stalk. He pulled the plant and found its fibrous root to be quite edible.

For thirty-seven days, Truman Everts traveled across the Yellowstone plateau, sustaining his life by eating thistle. His travels were not without incident. During one restless night in the geyser basin, his tossing and turning caused Everts to break through the thin geyserite crust, scalding his side from shoulder to hip. He spent one night in a tree while a mountain lion circled below him, screeching and hissing. Another night his campfire, lit by refracting sun through the lens of the opera glasses, blew up to engulf the forest around him in flame. He scorched his hand as he fled from the fire, the scars of which he bore for the rest of his life. Hallucinations from hunger and exhaustion took hold at times, and other times he collapsed on the ground in weary despair. He spent one full day retracing his steps, when he realized he had dropped his fire-starting lens during such a blackout. And when his spectacles broke, the nearsighted Everts could only recognize his food of choice, the thistle, by its spiny leaves.

Everts's traveling companions had not forgotten him. They retraced their steps, caching food and supplies in various places and tacking notes to trees. After spending several days looking for him, and being caught in the same snowstorm that had trapped Everts for ten days, the group was running low on supplies. Eventually they decided they must leave the park. When they returned to Montana, they hired two local men to return to the park and find Everts or, as they suspected, retrieve his body. On their first day in the park, Jack Baronette spotted a black bear in the distance. Since killing black bears was common practice in those days, Baronette raised his rifle to shoot the animal. As he focused the sight of the rifle on the bear, Baronette realized it was not a bear he was looking at, but the hunched over figure of a human being. They had found Truman Everts.

His rescuers reported that when Everts was found his flesh had wasted away and he weighed no more than eighty pounds. His belly swelled with thistle. Though the plant was edible, his digestive system was not able to break down its thick fibers. The material built up in his stomach, giving him a sense of satiation. Baronette, being a resourceful mountain man, went out and killed a bear. He took a pint of the bear's fat and forced it down the throat of his exhausted, delirious patient. The fat slicked up the thistle fibers, washing them out of Everts's system and replenishing his depleted energy supply. Apparently the remedy worked, for the next day Everts was ready to head home. He lived another thirty years after his adventure in Yellowstone. Rescue Creek, which flows through the northern part of the present-day park, was named for the miraculous rescue of a man everyone assumed to be dead. And the thistle that kept Everts alive during his perilous journey, commonly called elk thistle, was renamed Everts Thistle after the man who has perhaps eaten more of the plant than anyone since.

TO EAT OR NOT TO EAT?

If you had to survive in the Yellowstone wilderness without granola bars or instant oatmeal or any other food from home, would you know what you could eat? There are many healthy and tasty foods growing around Yellowstone, but there are also many others that would do more damage than good. Here are a few things to keep in mind when eating wild plants in Yellowstone, or anywhere else for that matter.

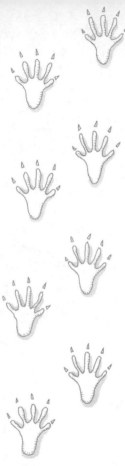

- Shun the 'shrooms. Though mushrooms are a tempting and familiar food, more than half the mushrooms found in Yellowstone—or anywhere—are extremely poisonous. Eating them can be fatal. Remember that many mushrooms look similar, so unless you are absolutely certain the mushroom you are holding is safe, don't take the chance. The odds aren't in your favor.

- Cut out carrots. If you have grown your own carrots, you may recognize many plants in Yellowstone from the carrot family. Their wispy tops and large root systems are distinct and friendly looking. However, most of the plants in this family are highly toxic. At least two people have died in Yellowstone by eating Water Hemlock.

- Be picky picking berries. Some berries in Yellowstone are tasty and sweet, others are sour and unpleasant, and still others are deadly. Don't eat berries unless you know what you are eating.

- Preserve the park. Remember that in Yellowstone it is illegal to pick plants and flowers, unless for *immediate* consumption. If you need food, don't hesitate to eat what you need to survive, but do so carefully. Be familiar with some life-sustaining plants in case you should need to use them. But it is much wiser to carry extra granola bars so you don't have to gamble on finding just the right edible plant.

Chapter Four

History

It was at noon camp in Hayden Valley that we gathered . . . fir cones and made [a] fire to boil our coffee . . . and cook our eggs. Strange, what a flavor there is to such simple experiences. I shall always love [that] spot even though I [shall] never see it again.

—*Margaret Andrews Cruikshank*[1]

Because so many of our memories are entwined with food, our history blends with tastes and flavors of the past. Food has always been an important part of a visit to Yellowstone, for nomadic tribes who summered in Yellowstone to hunt and gather roots and berries, as well as for early tourists who shed dusty robes in favor of elegant gowns for banquets at the Old Faithful Inn. Even simple acts like cooking coffee and eggs over a fire in Hayden Valley contribute to the memory of a place.

Not every food memory is pleasant. Some are comical, others are ironic, and some are even a bit sad. Their combination, however, creates a portrait of Yellowstone's past that is both intriguing and full of flavor.

The Yellowstone Supermarket

Today most people travel to Yellowstone to see geysers and hot springs, not to think about food. In the past, however, food was one of the biggest draws to the Yellowstone area. For hundreds of years, Native Americans have been traveling to Yellowstone to hunt and collect plants for eating and healing. These long trips to the "grocery store" lasted weeks or months. As the snow melted, different groups moved up onto the plateau for the summer to gather medicinal herbs, chip tools out of obsidian, fish the streams, and hunt elk and bison. Most of these groups moved on to lower elevations before the snow began to fall, carrying what they could to help them through the winter.

Buffalo Jerky Strips

There was an old saying around the stockyards of Chicago that when a pig was taken to slaughter, the butcher could "use everything but the squeal." Joe Medicine Crow, a Crow anthropologist and historian, says that his people did better than that in their use of the bison, for they used all of its vocalizations in their ceremonies and dances.

The American bison represented life for Native Americans residing on the Great Plains and westward. When horses came to their societies, nomadic groups could better follow and hunt the animal, increasing their dependency on the bison, not just for meat, but for tools, clothes, shelter, and even play. They sewed together buffalo hides to build their lodges, or tepees. They carved needles from bone. They carried everything from water to seeds in containers made of horn. Children even swiped buffalo ribs to make ice skates for winter play. No part of the animal went unused.

In order for buffalo-dependent societies to survive long winters and times when hunts were unsuccessful, they had to preserve the meat of the hunt. Curing the meat helped it to last several months, and also made it lighter and easier to carry. In many groups, women processed the spoils of the hunt, cutting the meat into strips for curing and tanning the hides for other uses. It was strenuous labor, especially if done with dull tools. A sharp obsidian blade, often acquired from Yellowstone directly or through trade, was a treasured tool for tanning and processing the meat.

Today, we eat preserved meat in the form of "jerky." We often buy these flavorful strips of beef at convenience stores, but you can make jerky from many meats in your own kitchen. Look for buffalo steaks at your supermarket or butcher shop, or use beef if you can't find buffalo.

Buffalo Jerky Strips

1 pound buffalo steak

3 teaspoons salt

1 teaspoon pepper

1 teaspoon chili powder

1 teaspoon garlic powder

1 teaspoon onion powder

1 teaspoon lemon pepper

¼ cup Worcestershire sauce

¼ cup soy sauce

Freeze meat until ice crystals form (30–60 minutes) for easier slicing. Cut meat diagonally across the grain, about ⅛ inch thick.

Spoon seasonings, including sauces, into a large, resealable plastic bag. Blend by massaging with fingers.

Place strips of buffalo in the bag, seal tightly, and shake until meat is coated with the seasonings. Marinate overnight.

Coat a large baking pan with aluminum foil and place a wire baking rack in the center. Lay meat strips across baking rack. Transfer pan and rack into the oven, leaving the door open slightly for moisture to escape.

Bake in oven at 250 degrees up to eight hours (or follow instruction manual if using an automatic food dehydrator). Meat should be chewy and still bendable. Store jerky in plastic bags or sealed containers.

THE BUFFALO HUNT

Hunting buffalo was an important ritual in the lives of Native Americans living on the Great Plains and Rocky Mountains. Not only was the hunt necessary for survival, but it was also a religious and cultural ceremony that united the community and gave young warriors opportunities to prove themselves and earn status in the tribe.

Hunters used a variety of weapons, including spears with obsidian heads and bows and arrows. While a decent bow could be crafted from bison horns the best bows available came from Yellowstone. By soaking the long, curled horn of the bighorn sheep in the mineral-rich hot springs, one could craft a bow strong enough to shoot an arrow right through a bison.

Arrows shot from bighorn bows have been timed (using modern equipment) at speeds of 150 feet per second. Such a strong bow was a valuable trade item for tribes who accessed the Yellowstone area.

Buffalo jumps, when available, were also used for hunting bison. A buffalo jump can be created on a cliff anywhere from 10 to 100 feet high. A warrior draped in calfskin danced near the brink of the cliff to lure in the herd. Other hunters lurked behind bushes in a rough V shape. As the herd approached the cliff, the hunters would rise up with shouts and hollers and drive the animals toward the edge, where they were unable to stop as the rest of the herd pressed up behind. Such jumps were an effective way of providing massive amounts of meat to sustain a community. Buffalo jumps provided so much meat that much of the animal could not be used or preserved before the meat spoiled. Deposits of bones at the bases of cliffs tell archeologists of the ancient uses of such brinks. But cliffs of any size are rare on the Great Plains, so most bison were hunted individually.

STICKY BERRY PUDDING

The summer berry season provided welcome variation to Native American diets. Yellowstone "shoppers" collected berries in abundance and often dried them for use during the winter. A mixture of dried meat and berries called *pemmican* was a staple winter supply. Bits of meat and

berries were stuck together with melted fat to form a large blob, which could be stored in a leather pouch. Not only could dried foods last through the winter, but they also had the advantage of being much lighter to carry. Throughout the year, cooks cut chunks of pemmican off as needed, perhaps to make a quick winter soup by dropping a chunk of pemmican in boiling water.

A favorite berry treat, however, was a sticky pudding made by boiling and mashing berries. While the pudding could be made out of any type of berry, chokecherries were a favorite. This bitter fruit gets its name because eating it makes you pucker, stimulating a choking reflex. You can make your pudding with chokecherries, but you might find the hard seeds difficult to palate. Furthermore, the seeds contain hydrocyanic acid which can be toxic eaten raw. If using chokecherries, boil the berries first, then strain the seeds before mashing.

Historically, honey would have been used where available to sweeten the mix, and ground arrowroot to thicken the sauce. This recipe has been adapted using cornstarch as the thickener, and sugar as the sweetener. While this pudding might once have been eaten plain or served like jam over bread items, the descendents of Yellowstone's berry-gathering tribes suggest pouring it over ice cream.

Sticky Berry Pudding

2 pounds berries (chokecherry, strawberry, blueberry)	1 cup sugar
2 cups water	1 tablespoon cornstarch

Wash and mash berries (if using chokecherries or larger fruit like peaches, boil the fruit before mashing). Put mashed fruit in a pan with 1 ½ cups water and sugar to taste. Bring the mixture slowly to a boil, then remove from heat. In a separate bowl, combine ½ cup water with cornstarch, mixing well. Add the cornstarch to the berry mixture, stirring constantly to prevent lumps from forming. Return to stove and heat on low setting until thickened, stirring frequently. Serve warm when mixture reaches the consistency of pudding.

YELLOWSTONE TEA

When you look in your medicine cabinet, you probably see a collection of pills and syrups claiming to calm a cold or lower a fever. Each bottle's label describes in detail exactly what this medicine should be used for: take this for coughing, this for allergies. Historically, however, one had to learn which plants, and parts of plants, could be used to treat an illness or injury. Native American tribes revered skilled healers who not only knew which plants to use, but where and when to find them. Under the direction of the healer, members of the tribes spent part of their Yellowstone summer replenishing the "first aid kit," collecting the plants that would be used to soothe aches and pains during the coming year.

Numerous herbal remedies can be found in Yellowstone, some powerful tonics and others calming teas. By gathering herbs and berries from your own backyard or supermarket, you can brew a Yellowstone Tea rich with the flavors and promises of health sought by the generations of healers.

Yellowstone Tea

Boil 4 cups water in a saucepan or tea kettle.

Add one of the collections of ingredients below.

Turn off the heat and let the tea steep about 5–15 minutes.

Pour into mugs, using a tea strainer if desired to remove leaves.

Sweeten with honey, about 1 tablespoon per cup, or to taste.

Mint/berry Tea:

> ½ cup crushed berries
>
> Handful fresh mint leaves (at least 12 good-size leaves)

Evergreen Tea:

> Handful pine needles (in spring, pine flowers and candles may also be used)
>
> 1 teaspoon cinnamon
>
> ½ teaspoon nutmeg

Note: This tea must steep twenty minutes to overnight. The water will turn a reddish color. Evergreen tea is rich in vitamin C but should be consumed in moderation, as large amounts can cause a bellyache. Pregnant women should not drink this tea.

Sagebrush Tea:

Handful sagebrush, including leaves and stems, chopped

Note: Sagebrush tea is very bitter, so add more sugar if desired. If the tea is simmered instead of steeped, it will be much stronger. This tea is popularly used for treating colds and other illness as it "brings out a sweat."

MEDICINAL USES OF SOME YELLOWSTONE PLANTS

Gathering plants in Yellowstone is illegal, unless being used individually for immediate consumption. Any plant should be positively identified before ingesting. Do not attempt to create extreme medicinal remedies without thorough understanding of the plant and its properties. Many plants that have edible parts also have toxic parts, and eating them can be fatal.

Curlycup gumweed/resinweed (grindelia squarrosa): *If you tangle with the curlycup gumweed you will quickly become familiar with the sticky "gum" that gives the plant its common name. Native Americans in the Northwest pounded resin out of the flower heads to use as a salve for poison ivy outbreaks. Gumweed is also used to treat lung affectations like bronchitis, asthma, and whooping cough.* Look for the bright yellow flowers, about two inches in diameter, in disturbed areas, particularly along roads in the park.

Plains prickly-pear (opuntia polycantha): *Before the invention of sterile plastic strips and rubber bandages, playful children still suffered from skinned knees and elbows. What could you use to stop the bleeding? You might try a prickly-pear pad. When the spines are scraped off the pear-shaped stems, they can be sliced in half and the juicy interior applied to wounds. Lash the pad on with a strip of bark or woven grasses and you have a natural bandage—just be careful to remove all the spines before slapping the cactus to your skin.*

Prickly-pear fuzz was also used by the Blackfoot tribe to treat warts. Prickly-pear grow in the hottest, driest parts of Yellowstone, particularly at the low elevations in the north. Look for the cactus on the north entrance road between Mammoth Hot Springs and Gardiner, Montana. The bright yellow flowers appear in the late spring.

Prince's-Pine (chimaphila umbellate): *Medicine always goes down better if it tastes like candy, making tonics from prince's-pine an excellent choice for those who need that spoonful of sugar to get it down. Prince's-pine, or pipsissewa, has been used to flavor soft drinks and candy, but its high concentration of vitamin C gives it excellent medicinal properties as well. Studies suggest that drinking pipsissewa tea increases urine flow, effectively treating fluid retention and bladder problems. Its healing properties might also extend to milder fevers and coughs, as well as kidney infections.* The light pink and white, saucer-shaped flowers of this evergreen shrub stand out on the floors of coniferous forests. Look for clusters of five to eight small flowers, less than 1 cm across.

Self-heal (prunella vulgaris): *A plant with a name like "self-heal" has a lot to prove in the medicinal department. Self-heal has been used to treat a variety of ailments, from mouth sores to ulcers. A tea from the leaves was gargled for sore throats and drunk to ease stomachaches and diarrhea. A salve was spread on bruises, wounds, and insect bites. Contemporary research suggests that self-heal has antibiotic properties and contains urso-*

lic acid, a compound that works to heal tumors. Self-heal can also lower blood pressure. The purple flowers of this perennial herb grow in clusters at the top of short stems. The dense spikes of flowers bloom in July and August.

And what if you just had a headache that wouldn't go away? You could try chewing on the bark of an aspen or willow tree. Scientists have discovered salicylic acid in the bark of trees in the willow family. Today, salicylic acid is the active ingredient in aspirin.

Trappin' for Dinner

Nobody could weave a tale about the wonders of the Yellowstone like a trapper. These explorers followed the trail of stories passed on by the Native Americans up the Missouri and Yellowstone rivers to the heart of geyser country. There they found not only valuable beaver pelts, but natural treasures that could certainly make for a fanciful evening of storytelling. An exchange recorded by General Nelson A. Miles between himself and mountain man Jim Bridger has become an oft-quoted example of the trapper's flair for exaggeration. Says Miles,

> "But Jim, there are some things in this world besides beaver. I was down [in Arizona] last winter and saw great trees with limbs and bark all turned to stone."
>
> "O," returned Jim, "that's peetrifaction. Come with me to the Yellowstone next summer, and I'll show you peetrified trees a-growing, with petrified birds on 'em a-singing peetrified songs."[2]

One particularly embellished account even described the fruit on the trees.

> . . . and more wonderful still, these petrified bushes bear the most wonderful fruit—diamonds, rubies, sapphires, emeralds, etc., etc., as large as black walnuts, are found in abundance. "I tell you, sir," said one narrator, "it is true for I gathered a quart myself, and sent them down the country."[3]

Certainly, the thought of diamonds and rubies growing like fruit on trees appealed to folks back east, and stories like these added to the lure of Yellowstone and the West as a whole. Even in our modern kitchens we are unable to turn fruit to precious gems, but you can give your fruits a gem-like shine and rich flavor by turning them into Peetrified Apples.

Peetrified Apples

10 apples

10 Popsicle or wooden craft sticks

2 cups granulated sugar

1 cup light corn syrup

1 ½ cups water

5 drops red food coloring

2 drops cinnamon oil (optional)

Grease a large baking sheet. Wash apples and remove stems, then insert wooden craft sticks into whole apples.

Combine sugar, corn syrup, and water in a medium saucepan. Heat over medium-high to 300 degrees Fahrenheit. Use a candy thermometer to gauge temperature, or drop a small amount of syrup into a cup of cold water. If syrup hardens into brittle threads, the mixture is hot enough.

Remove from heat and add food coloring and cinnamon oil if desired. Stir until combined.

Holding each apple by its stick, dip into syrup and swirl to coat evenly. Pull out of syrup, briefly allowing excess syrup to drip from the apple and twisting excess strands onto the apple. Return to prepared cookie sheet and cool until hard.

FISH TALES

The trappers' fanciful tales weren't the only thing a bit "fishy" in their reports of Yellowstone. Travelers in the rugged west could not ignore the readily available heat source during their travels

GEYSER PLAY

These adventurous explorers couldn't resist a few "experiments" with the geysers—stories that received ample embellishment in the retelling. A young man, William Kennerly, traveling with the fur trader William Sublette in 1843, compared the hot springs he saw to an ice cream soda:

One geyser, a soda spring, was so effervescent that I believe the syrup to be the only thing lacking to make it equal a giant ice cream soda of the kind now popular at a drugstore. We tried some experiments with our first discovery by packing it down with armfuls of grass; then we placed a flat stone on top of that, on which four of us, joining hands, stood in a vain attempt

to hold it down. In spite of our efforts to curb Nature's most potent force, when the moment of necessity came, Old Steam Boat would literally rise to the occasion and throw us all high into the air like so many feathers. It inspired one with great awe for the wonderful works of the Creator to think that this had been going on with the regularity of clockwork for thousands of years, and the thought of our being almost the first white men to see it did not lessen its effect.[4]

It is unlikely that humans of any strength would be able to resist the surface force of a geyser eruption, even momentarily, and walk away from such an attempt unscalded. Kennerly's account seems appropriately classed among stories of "peetrified birds" singing "peetrified songs."

in the Yellowstone region, a perfect place for cooking dinner. With a bit less exaggeration than his geyser throttle story, Kennerly writes of geysers "so hot that we boiled our bacon in them, as well as the fine speckled trout which we caught in the surrounding streams."[5]

It seems the Washburn expedition of 1870 stumbled on the possibility of boiling fresh fish in the springs. This group of explorers traveled to the Yellowstone region to document and record the "truth" behind the Indian legends and trapper tales. They spent forty days in the area, mapping, climbing, and naming features along the way. Their reports would eventually prompt Congress to send Ferdinand Hayden, of the United States Geological Survey, on a series of official expeditions, thus beginning the national park movement.

Cornelius Hedges, a member of the Washburn expedition, was fishing along the shore of Yellowstone Lake near a hot spring. As he pulled a trout from the lake, the fish fell back into the spring. The trout swam frantically for a moment before rising, fully boiled, to the top. This occurrence, published in a magazine article a year later, probably occurred at Fishing Cone, a hot spring in the West Thumb geyser basin whose cone is often surrounded by the lake waters on all sides. The publicity of the account led to the popular notion of catching a fish in the lake, then swinging 180 degrees and dropping it into the spring to be cooked, literally, on the hook.

The Hayden expedition of 1871 records a repetition of this event at what they called Fish Pot. Soon Fishing Cone was on the Grand Loop tour. Visitors would pose for photographs on the cone wearing a chef's hat and apron. But cooking in a geyser is dangerous, as one fisherman learned in 1921 when he was scalded by the hot spring. Anglers during 1919 and 1939 also got a surprise when Fishing Cone erupted to heights of forty feet.

Today, cooking in hot springs is illegal for many reasons, including the potential harm to humans and the thermal features. Furthermore, toxic minerals such as arsenic and mercury have been found in the park's thermal waters, and being exposed to these and other minerals through the cooking process would be unhealthy.

Cone-Boiled Fish

3 whole trout
Water
1 cup apple cider vinegar

½ cup parsley
1 tablespoon lemon juice
Zest from one lemon

| 1 tablespoon salt | Lemon wedges |
| ½ cup butter | |

Clean fish well. Place whole in a kettle, filling with enough water to cover the fish. Add vinegar and salt. Bring to a boil, reduce heat, and simmer 10–15 minutes.

Cream butter. Chop parsley and add to butter. Squeeze and zest lemon, adding both to the butter mixture. Whip until light and fluffy.

Drain fish. Lift carefully and arrange on hot platter. Garnish platter with parsley sprigs and lemon wedges. Serve with parsley butter.

Yellowstone by Wagon

In 1872, President Ulysses S. Grant signed the act establishing Yellowstone as the first national park. While people across the nation applauded the decision to set aside a public park, the first years of the park's existence were quiet compared to what we know now. Yellowstone was remote and generally inaccessible to population centers in the eastern United States. Still, a few adventurers wandered into the new park, curious about the tall tales told by trappers returning from the West or lured to Yellowstone by the stunning paintings of Thomas Moran, who documented the exploratory expedition of 1871.

What might you have packed if your family had decided to vacation in Yellowstone in 1872? There were no hotels or campgrounds. You would probably sleep on a blanket or two inside a heavy canvas tent. You could have packed some gear in a wagon, but since there were no roads yet, much of your travel would be done on horseback. What food would you have brought from home? What would you count on finding in the park? In Yellowstone's earliest years, travelers could legally hunt for food in the park, so you would certainly have brought along rifles and fishing tackle. Bears were a concern even then, and without a vehicle to store your gear, you would certainly worry that a bear might gobble up all your food.

At that time, you might occasionally use hot springs for cooking, but you would probably find it more convenient to do your cooking over a fire. A big kettle was a must for heating water and cooking stews. You might also use a cast-iron pot heated with coals. These Dutch ovens are still used by campers for cooking over fires, and provide a great way to cook breads and rice out in the woods. As you dine on Cowboy Cornbread and Cheater's Upside-Down Cake, imagine the satisfaction of having a hot meal slow-cooked over the fire after a day exploring a brand-new national park.

Cowboy Cornbread

1 cup flour
1 cup cornmeal
½ teaspoon salt
3 teaspoons baking powder
1 medium onion, chopped
1 green chili (if desired), chopped,
   or one small can diced green chilies

1 can (12 ounces) creamed corn
10 sage leaves, chopped
½ cup pine nuts
2 eggs
1 cup milk
¼ cup butter, melted
Butter for Dutch oven or skillet

Mix flour, cornmeal, salt, and baking powder in a mixing bowl. In a second bowl, combine onion, chilies, creamed corn, sage leaves, and pine nuts. Mix well and add the corn mixture to

the dry ingredients and stir until incorporated. Using the bowl you just emptied, blend the eggs, milk, and melted butter. Combine all ingredients, stirring just until moistened.

To cook in Dutch oven:

Heat 20 charcoal briquettes in fire ring or on a grill. Position your 10-inch Dutch oven over half of the charcoal. Melt 2 tablespoons of butter in the bottom of the Dutch oven. Pour batter into oven, causing the melted butter to coat the bottom and sides of the oven, spilling over onto the top of the batter. Place the lid on the Dutch oven and move 12 coals to the lid. Bake about 25 minutes, or until a toothpick inserted in the center comes out clean.

To cook in skillet:

Preheat oven to 400 degrees. Place 2 tablespoons butter in a 10-inch, cast-iron skillet. Melt butter by placing skillet in oven for about 5 minutes. Remove from oven, swirling butter to coat skillet. Pour prepared batter into the skillet. Return to oven and bake about 20 minutes, until cooked in the center. Cool slightly before serving straight from the skillet.

Cheater's Upside-Down Cake

1 box yellow cake mix

1 can sliced pineapple, drained;
   reserve juice

3 eggs

¼ cup vegetable oil

⅓ cup butter, cut into ¼-inch cubes

¾ cup brown sugar

1 can sliced pineapple rings (10 slices),
   with juice

10 maraschino cherries

Prepare a 12-inch Dutch oven, lining with aluminum foil if desired.

In a mixing bowl or sealable freezer bag, combine cake mix, eggs, oil, and pineapple juice. Mix until smooth, adding a bit more water if needed.

Arrange pineapple rings in bottom of Dutch oven. Place a cherry in the center of each ring, and between rings until cherries are used up. Sprinkle pineapple with brown sugar, then dot with pieces of butter.

Pour cake batter over fruit mixture, spreading evenly. Place lid on Dutch oven and place over coals. Bake around 350 degrees (12–14 coals on top, 10–12 below) about 35 minutes. Test cake with a knife when edges begin to pull away from the sides of the Dutch oven. When cake is done, knife will come clean when removed.

Serve from Dutch oven or invert onto platter to serve upside down.

BUILDING YELLOWSTONE

The era of the lone and isolated trapper or traveler would not last long in the new national park. As Yellowstone matured into a tourist destination, crews of engineers and builders came to build roads and buildings. These groups of workers lived in tent camps that moved where the work was. They received $1.75 in wages plus food. Meals were simple but hearty for the laborers. One day's menu at an 1892 camp listed the following:

Breakfast: oatmeal, bread, beef steak, baked potatoes, and coffee

Lunch: soup, corned beef and cabbage, boiled potatoes, onions, bread, and coffee

Supper: hash, bread, fruit, and tea

One cook, who fed a camp of engineers for several summers, built a reputation for varying the drab fare with fresh vegetables and even homemade donuts. Bill Brumington's donuts were a hot commodity in his camp. One evening, he distributed a donut to each worker as a bedtime snack. He saved a second round of the fried bread for breakfast, covering them in big bowl on the kitchen table. When Bill awoke in the morning, he discovered an empty bowl where his donuts had been. Furious at the gluttony of the workmen, Bill refused to talk to any of them for days. He was the one eating his words, however, when they broke camp for their next move. When they pulled up the floorboards from the kitchen tent, they found a stash of stale donuts, tucked away for the winter by a hungry pack rat.

Brumington Donuts

2 eggs

1 cup sugar

1 cup milk

¼ teaspoon salt

2 tablespoons melted butter or margarine

1 teaspoon vanilla

3 cups flour

3 teaspoons baking powder

¼ teaspoon nutmeg

¼ teaspoon cinnamon

Oil for frying

Beat eggs. Add sugar, milk, salt, butter, and vanilla. Blend until smooth. Gradually add flour, baking powder and spices. Add enough flour to make a stiff batter, thick enough to hold a spoon in standing position.

Heat oil to 365 degrees. Prepare a plate with three paper towels for draining the cooked donuts. Fill a small bowl with granulated sugar, powdered sugar, or a sugar combination such as cinnamon and sugar or powdered and granulated sugars (for better "stick"). Set the sugar bowl between the towel-lined plate and a serving platter.

Carefully drop batter by spoonfuls into hot oil, a few at a time (children should not attempt this step, as oil will splash when dough is dropped in). Fry until lightly browned. The donuts will usually turn themselves as they cook in the oil, but if a lopsided donut has trouble turning, use a fork to help it along. When browned, gently remove donuts from the oil and place on paper towels to drain.

After donuts have cooled a few moments, drop into sugar mixture and roll to coat on all sides (this is a great job for young chefs). Transfer from sugar mixture to serving platter, and try to keep them away from eager hands long enough to finish cooling.

Fry as many donuts as you want to eat now, then refrigerate the remaining dough to be fried later and eaten fresh.

YELLOWSTONE BY STAGE

With new roads and hotels, the wonders of Yellowstone became evermore accessible to curious travelers. In 1883 the Northern Pacific Railroad opened a line right up to the park's north entrance. From there, visitors were handed over to the Yellowstone Park Company, who loaded them onto stagecoaches to begin a grand tour of the park. After a night in the Mammoth Hotel and time spent exploring the Mammoth Hot Springs, visitors climbed back in the stagecoaches for a five-

day Grand Loop tour, bumping along dusty park roads during the day, then trading in their traveling clothes for ballroom attire and a night of dining and dancing at one of the elegant hotels.

HIGHWAY ROBBERY TRUFFLES

Travelers on the Grand Loop tour faced a variety of hazards as they wound around the park roads. Steep grades and crowds of agitated horses often caused stagecoach accidents. While drivers and passengers eagerly swapped terrifying accounts of bolting horses and stages sliding down steep embankments, the most lavishly embellished tales were those of highway robbery.

Though stories of gunmen with masks and gangs with pistols proliferated around Yellowstone campfires, only five holdups were officially documented during the stagecoach era. Both the biggest and the last stagecoach robberies of the twentieth century were reputed to have occurred in Yellowstone National Park. As automobiles had already replaced stagecoaches through most of the country, it is indeed possible that the last stagecoach robbery in the West was the July 9, 1915, robbery of five stages just south of Madison Junction. The highwayman looted just $200 from passengers before he was spotted and the army was called in. He escaped into the woods and was never arrested for the crime. Bernard Baruch, a respected statesman and presidential adviser, was riding that particular stage. Thrilled by the real-life frontier adventure, he remarked that the day's entertainment was "the best $50 I ever spent." Of course, Baruch had earned millions of dollars on the New York Stock Exchange by the time he was thirty.

A few bandits made out a little better in the cash department. A 1908 robbery, hyped as the greatest holdup of the century, struck twenty-five coaches and wagons on a hairpin curve south of Old Faithful. This distance between the coaches was just enough that one stage after another fell into the trap. After stripping the passengers and drivers of their valuables, the robber walked away with over $2,000 in money and jewelry—and a sweet snack on the side. A girl sitting next to the driver on one of the wagons was carrying a box of chocolates on her lap. Seeing the box, the robber asked what was inside. She told him it was candy, to which he replied, "Well, give me some." He helped himself to two pieces before moving on to the next wagon. Even in the chaos of highway robbery, it seems there is always time for chocolate.

Highway Robbery Truffles

1 ½ pounds chocolate   Peppermint oil or vanilla extract

1 cup heavy cream

Heat oven to lowest temperature (110°) and then turn off.

Chop chocolate into chunks about the size of golf balls. Put chocolate in small mixing bowl, then place in warm oven until melted, stirring occasionally.

In a small saucepan or in a microwave, heat cream to lukewarm.

Add cream to chocolate all at once. Beat with electric mixer, slowly at first to prevent splattering. Beat 30 seconds to 1 minute, until well mixed.

Add either ½ teaspoon vanilla or 3–5 drops oil of peppermint (not spearmint). Beat until flavor is blended.

Pour truffles into buttered 9-inch pan. Chill in refrigerator for at least twelve hours. For best results, chill 2–3 days.

Cut into bite-size squares and serve straight from the pan. Or, for a flair irresistible to highway-men, scoop truffles from the pan by spoonfuls, then roll between clean hands to form a round ball. Drop the gooey ball into a bowl of dark baking cocoa and roll until coated on all sides. When well coated, lift the ball from the cocoa and place in a decorative candy cup to serve.

Lemonade Springs

One of the first stops on a stagecoach trip into Yellowstone was a spring called Apollinaris. The name was an ironic reference to a famous brand of mineral water, which was (and is to this day) imported from Germany. A shrewd marketer managed to convince travelers that none of the water in the park was drinkable. Travelers stocked up on bottles of Apollinaris and other waters to carry throughout their journey. When empty, these bottles were tossed out of stage-coach windows to lie on the side of the road. Stagecoach drivers called these empties "dead soldiers."

Some drivers, wanting to convince their passengers that they had been duped, pulled off at Apollinaris Spring, where they filled their bottles with cold mineral water from the spring. Visitors quickly began to catch onto the ruse. In 1890, Carter Harrison gave name to the spring, and described his experience drinking from its waters:

Guide books tell us not to drink the water. I think their writers were in collusion with the hotel man-agement to force guests to buy lager and apollinaris at 50 cents a bottle. By the way, there is on the first days drive an apollinaris spring. It seems to me the simon pure thing. We drank freely of it at the spring and afterwards from bottles carried for several hours. One of the bottles was tightly corked, and, when opened, popped as if well charged.[6]

As the automobile replaced the stage, Apollinaris remained an immensely popular attraction. Some travelers remember mixing water from Apollinaris with flavored beverage mixes for a bubbly drink. The water is slightly fizzy due to traces of carbon dioxide gas coming up with the liquid. Carbon dioxide is used today to carbonate water for soda and other beverages. When you make Lemonade Springs you create the chemical reaction that releases carbon dioxide by combining acidic lemon juice with baking soda.

Lemonade Springs

2-quart pitcher of water   3 tablespoons sugar

2 teaspoons baking soda   2 tablespoons lemon juice

Pour the baking soda and sugar into the pitcher of water, stirring until completely dissolved.

Add the lemon juice.

Watch as the lemon juice reacts with the baking soda to produce carbon dioxide gas (CO_2). You can see the carbon dioxide escaping in the form of tiny bubbles. The gases coming out of geysers in Yellowstone really are like the bubbles that make your soda carbonated. Now pour yourself a glass from your own lemonade springs and enjoy a bubbly lemon drink.

HOTELS

The railroad companies had their eyes on Yellowstone, knowing that if they could build a railroad line to the park they could lure a whole new group of people to see the "Wonders of the Yellowstone." In 1883 the first hotel, called the National Hotel, was built in Yellowstone National Park. Twenty-one years later, Robert Reamur's architectural masterpiece, the Old Faithful Inn, was opened for business.

The Yellowstone Park Company promoted a five-day tour of the Yellowstone Park. Visitors would arrive by the Northern Pacific Railroad in the north, where they were met and escorted to the hotel in Mammoth Hot Springs. The next day they embarked on a stagecoach journey through the park, stopping at the feature attractions and spending every night in the luxurious accommodations of grand hotels.

The hotels themselves became as much a part of the Yellowstone experience as geysers and grizzly bears. Every night, visitors would shake off their dusty travel clothes and don elegant evening wear. After a multicourse meal, tables would be cleared and the floors opened up for dancing. The music played long into the night until weary travelers retired to rest for another day of geyser gazing and bumpy stagecoach rides.[7]

Veal Cutlet with Paprika Sauce

1 ½-pound veal round	4 cups bread crumbs
4 eggs	Salt and pepper to taste

1 tablespoon Worcestershire sauce   ½ pound butter
2 cups all-purpose flour

Slice veal round into 8 3-ounce pieces. Pound with meat hammer until ⅛ inch thick. Scramble eggs in bowl with Worcestershire. Pour flour and bread crumbs into a separate, shallow, flat container (a pie pan would work fine). Season veal with salt and pepper, dredge in flour, dip in egg, and then dredge in breadcrumbs. Make sure each step is well coated. Melt butter in sauté pan and fry breaded veal until golden brown. Serve with paprika sauce.

August 8, 1922

Paprika Sauce

1 large yellow onion   3 tablespoons paprika
¼ cup vegetable oil   1 cup sour cream
¼ cup all-purpose flour   Salt and pepper to taste
1 pint chicken or veal stock

Cut onion into julienne strips and sauté in vegetable oil until translucent. Dust with flour and stir to combine. Add cold stock and paprika and bring to a boil then let simmer 15 minutes. Finish with sour cream and salt and pepper.

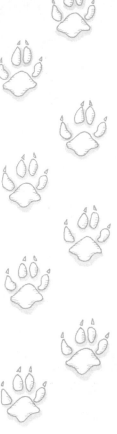

Pan-Fried Rocky Mountain Trout with Hazelnut Butter

4 trout fillets, 5 ounces each

Salt and pepper to taste

½ cup milk

1 cup all-purpose flour

4 ounces clarified butter

2 ounces whole butter

2 ounces hazelnuts rough chopped

4 tablespoons lemon juice

2 tablespoons chopped parsley

Season trout with salt and pepper. Dip the fish in the milk and dredge in flour. Sauté the trout in clarified butter. Remove and keep warm. Pour off the extra butter in the pan. Add the whole butter and let brown slightly. Add the hazelnuts and cook until lightly toasted. Add lemon juice and parsley and pour over fish.

July 25, 1934

Fried Spring Chicken with Cream Gravy

2 whole chickens, no more than
   3 ½ pounds each

4 cups all-purpose flour

1 tablespoon ground thyme

1 tablespoon ground sage

1 tablespoon ground tarragon

Salt and pepper to taste

4 quarts shortening

Split chickens in half and remove backbone and thighbones. Mix flour through salt and pepper. Dredge chicken pieces in flour mixture. Heat shortening to 350 degrees, using a candy thermometer to test. Make sure your pot is large enough to handle the volume of the chicken and shortening with at least six inches to spare. When oil has reached temperature submerge chicken in oil and cook until an internal temperature of 160 degrees is reached. Remove from oil and let rest for five minutes before serving with cream gravy.

July 4, 1947

Cream Gravy

4 tablespoons butter	½ cup dry white wine
6 ounces chicken livers, rinsed	½ cup chicken stock
3 ounces minced onion	2 cups heavy cream
4 tablespoons all-purpose flour	Salt and pepper to taste

Sauté onions and livers in butter two minutes. Add flour and stir. Add cold wine, stock, and heavy cream, bring to a boil, then let simmer 15 minutes. Puree sauce in blender or with an immersion blender. Strain. Adjust seasoning and consistency.

DEVIL'S KITCHENETTE

While the hotel business was booming, some other visitors were getting impatient. Those who couldn't afford to stay in the hotels were left to fend for themselves while traveling through the

NOT SO PLEASANT IN PLEASANT VALLEY

The northeast corner of Yellowstone was one of the last areas to enter the stagecoach route. The development area near Tower Falls began as a stopover point for miners traveling to or from Cooke City and a few folks fishing the Yellowstone River. The first hotel at Tower claimed to accommodate up to twenty guests in its five rooms. John Yancey, the proprietor, advertised "excellent accommodations for tourists and travelers," though many guests of the Pleasant Valley Hotel seemed to disagree.

Major John Pitcher, in a letter sent to "Uncle John" Yancey in May 1902 wrote,

I am aware of the fact that it is not an easy matter for you to run a first class restaurant or table at your hotel, on account of your isolated position and distance from the railroad, but you certainly can improve on your arrangements of last summer. You have an attractive place, and in your own interests I should suggest that you make some changes and improvements in the fare which you offer travelers and tourists.[8]

Perhaps travelers had right to complain. Typical and unvarying fare at Yancey's place was bacon, eggs, and fish fried in rancid butter. The single variation was rare slices of raw Bermuda onion, which Uncle John said was "good for the narvs." Meals and board ran for $2 per day or $10 per week.

park. Stories abound of the Yellowstone Park Company's hotels refusing to so much as sell an independent traveler a bottle of milk.

Two enterprising women recognized these less wealthy, but still enthusiastic, travelers as a potential market. Anna Pryor and Elizabeth Trischman opened their first general store and soda fountain in Mammoth Hot Springs in 1916. Eight years later, they erected a snack stand near a popular feature on the Upper Terraces of Mammoth. This feature, a travertine cave that could be entered from above via a long wooden ladder, was called the Devil's Kitchen. Pryor and Trischman called their stand, appropriately, the Devil's Kitchenette. The stand operated for six years, selling soda and other treats, until the cave was determined to be unsafe for touring, due to lethal gases trapped in the cavern. The Devil's Kitchen and Kitchenette both closed to business in 1930.

Ice Cream Sodas from the Devil's Kitchenette

¼ cup cold, vitamin D milk

4 tablespoons chocolate syrup

2 scoops chocolate or vanilla ice cream

1 cup seltzer water or club soda

Chill a tall, 12-ounce glass in the freezer. When frosty, fill with milk and chocolate syrup. Stir briskly to mix.

Add one scoop ice cream and a squirt of seltzer. Mash gently.

Add second scoop of ice cream. Fill glass to brim with seltzer.

Stir gently until bubbles form on top.

Insert straw and serve with a long-handled spoon.

LIVING AND WORKING IN YELLOWSTONE

When Yellowstone National Park was signed into existence in 1872, Congress appropriated no funds for its management. Within a decade, however, it became clear that someone needed to establish and maintain some sort of order in the park. Poachers were slaughtering wildlife, buildings were popping up randomly around the park, and visitation was slowly creeping up. In 1886, the United States called in the cavalry. On August 13, Company M of the 1st U.S. Cavalry marched into Mammoth Hot Springs and immediately made its presence known. Trails were patrolled. Arrests were made. Neat and orderly buildings were put up, while ugly and unsafe buildings were torn down. The army, it seemed, was here to stay.

The military established its headquarters in the vicinity of the Mammoth Hot Springs. The first building erected at Fort Yellowstone was a guardhouse, then a neat row of officers' quarters and a bunkhouse for the soldiers. Soldiers created a parade ground by hauling thousands of tons of topsoil onto the white travertine terraces that cover the Mammoth area. Neatly trimmed lawns were planted over dry sagebrush flats, enticing the Mammoth elk herd down to the fort to graze on juicy green grasses.

Most of the soldiers were required to live in the bunkhouses, leaving wives and families behind, but officers brought their families to Fort Yellowstone. The three-story homes on officers' row provided ample accommodations for families, including quarters in the attic for a maid who worked for the household cleaning and preparing the meals.

Fort Yellowstone was a social place. When they could get away with it, soldiers would socialize with female hotel employees, stealing them from under the noses of jealous stagecoach drivers. Holidays, in particular, were a festive time around the fort. George Henderson records the following account of a Fort Yellowstone Christmas, perhaps not too different from our modern holiday celebrations:

> The ladies of Fort Yellowstone united in making Christmas a joyful occasion for the Sunday School children. The Christmas tree was brilliantly illuminated and bore an abundance of that fruit which children most desire. Captain Brown made one of the jolliest Saints that ever distributed dolls to the outstretched arms of baby-mothers, so eager to kiss and embrace them. The boys were in raptures over their horns, tin horses, soldiers and locomotives. All were sweetened up to the highest degree ever indicated by any saccarimeters, boys and girls being most accurate ones. When the tree was cleared of its fruit the jolly Saint informed his patrons that there were millions more expecting to see him that night and that he must bid them farewell. . . . The hoary-headed Saint vanished, surrounded by a halo of glory in the minds of the children, and that he was no mere illusion was evident from the fact that arms and pockets were full of dolls, candies and many other good things. Mrs. W. E. Wilder, although suffering from a sprained ankle, was present and furnished the music to which the school children marched and sang in joyful concert.[9]

KEEPING INN FOR A WINTER WONDERLAND

Food becomes scarce during the Yellowstone winter for animals and humans alike. Trapped by snowbanks and winter storms, winter residents rarely get to venture into the border towns for groceries, so fresh produce becomes a welcome addition to a diet of canned and dried foods.

GUESS WHAT'S FOR DINNER?

Wintering in a backcountry patrol cabin was a lonely detail for young soldiers in Yellowstone. In preparation for the winter, soldiers spent many weeks chopping firewood and hauling in supplies from the border towns. Before the first snow fell, they had to bring in several months worth of food by horseback so the cabin would be ready for use when the patrolman arrived for the season.

Regulations prohibited soldiers from bringing anyone with them into the backcountry, and a winter spent patrolling the wilderness in search of poachers could get mighty lonely at times. Stories abound of soldiers smuggling their wives into the backcountry for the winter, then smuggling them out before the snow melted in the springtime.

Single soldiers found amusements as well. One soldier arrived for the winter at his cabin, which had been prepared by other patrolmen. When he opened his cupboards he found that his rambunctious comrades had removed all the labels from his canned provisions. For the entire winter, he began every meal wondering whether he would be dining on peaches or pork 'n' beans.

Buelah Brown spent a winter in the 1920s with the Musser family, innkeepers at Old Faithful. After eleven winters in the park, the Mussers had learned how to supplement their winter diet. By channeling water from a small geyser near the inn, they were able to heat their house and water; they also kept a small chicken house and greenhouse.

HIGH ON THE HOG

Dull army rations were supplemented by creative food exchanges between soldiers and travelers. Fresh produce had an ever-increasing market value as one moved deeper into the park. One year the officers bought young pigs for soldiers stationed in the interior. Bored soldiers quickly adopted these pigs as pets. When it came time to butcher the pigs for meat, the soldiers had to swap pigs among neighboring stations, so nobody had to kill or eat the pig he had raised.

Brown delighted in having fresh vegetables throughout the winter, bragging about the two-foot-long cucumbers grown in the greenhouse and the superb flavor of geyser-watered produce:

> I wish you might have tasted the radishes; I mention these especially because they were without doubt supernaturally delicious. The lettuce, onions and tomatoes were more than appreciated. I often wished that the outside world could look in and be jealous when they would see our combination salads.[10]

Today, no thermal water is used in the park for heating buildings, watering plants, or warming bath water. This historic practice destroyed the geysers and hot springs from which water was taken. In order to preserve all thermal features in their natural state, the buildings and bathwater in Yellowstone are now heated the same way buildings and bathwater are heated in Los

Angeles, California, or Johnson City, Tennessee. When the snow falls at Old Faithful this year, there won't be a greenhouse to supply fresh greens through the winter. As the months drag on and employees dig deeper into their reserves of canned peas and corn, crisp lettuce will be but a memory. Employees report that the rare vegetable carried into the park in the pouch of someone's snowmobile can be sold for ten times its purchase price when it reaches Old Faithful. Imagine what you could get for a fresh, green salad like Buelah Brown's . . .

OLD FAITHFUL WINTER SALAD

½ pound bacon

½ cup mayonnaise

2 teaspoons red wine vinegar

¼ cup fresh basil, finely chopped

4 slices French bread

1 teaspoon salt

1 teaspoon ground black pepper

canola oil

1 pound romaine lettuce, washed and dried

3 green onions, chopped

1 pint cherry tomatoes, quartered

2 hardboiled eggs, sliced

Cook bacon. Drain and cool, then crumble into small bits. Set aside.

Reserve 2 tablespoons of bacon drippings. Whisk drippings, mayonnaise, vinegar, and basil. Cover and let stand at room temperature.

Cut French bread into ½ inch cubes. In a large skillet, toss bread pieces with salt and pepper. Drizzle with canola oil and cook over medium heat until golden brown. Remove from heat.

In a large bowl, tear lettuce into bite-sized pieces. Toss with onions, tomatoes, bacon, bread pieces, and salad dressing. Garnish with egg slices.

AN UNINVITED DINNER GUEST

Living in a national park is a life unlike any other. Residents awake in the morning to the sound of elk bugling or bison steps on the front porch. "I got stuck in a bear jam" is a valid excuse for being late for work. And water-cooler gossip revolves around the sighting of a rare butterfly or whether a certain bear was seen creeping through the campground last night.

In the early 1960s, Inger Garrison, wife of the Yellowstone superintendent, learned that cooking in Yellowstone is also full of surprises. Garrison took pride in the gourmet meals she managed to throw together in spite of her wilderness surroundings. On one occasion she was preparing a dinner for the director of the National Park Service, baking fresh cinnamon rolls and preparing trays of fruits, vegetables, and hors d'oeuvres. After stepping out for a few moments to collect the mail, Garrison returned to her kitchen to find the building turned upside down. The trays were licked clean, the bread was scattered, and the refrigerator was open and empty, its contents strewn over the floor. Tracks in the flour led to the second floor, where the intruder was apprehended—a 400-pound black bear with guilty puffs of flour on his snout.

Notes

1. Margaret Andrews Cruikshank, "A Lady's Trip to Yellowstone, 1883; 'Earth could not furnish another such sight,'" ed. Lee H. Whittlesey, *Montana* 39, no. 1: 13.

2. Nelson A. Miles, *Personal Recollections and Observations of General Nelson A. Miles* (Chicago: Werner, 1897), 137.

3. William F. Raynolds, *The Report of Brevet Brigadier General W. F. Raynolds on the Exploration of the Yellowstone and the Country Drained by that River,* 40th Congress., 1st sess., Sen. Ex. Doc. no. 77, July 17, 1868, p. 77. Cited in Aubrey L. Haines, *Yellowstone National Park: Its Exploration and Establishment* (Washington: U.S. Department of the Interior, 1974), 20.

4. William Clark Kennerly, *Persimmon Hill: A Narrative of Old St. Louis* (Norman: University of Oklahoma Press, 1948), 156–57. Cited in Haines, *Yellowstone National Park,* 17–18.

5. Kennerly, *Persimmon Hill,* 156.

6. Cited in Lee H. Whittlesey, *Yellowstone Place Names* (Helena: Montana Historical Society Press, 1988).

7. Hotel recipes courtesy Xanterra Parks and Resorts in Yellowstone National Park, Jim Chapman, executive chef.

8. John Pitcher, letters sent, 11:396, YNP Archives. Cited in Aubrey Haines, *The Yellowstone Story* (Niwot: University Press of Colorado, 1996), 2:241.

9. Cited in Aubrey Haines, *The Yellowstone Story: A History of Our First National Park* (Boulder: University Press of Colorado, 1996), 181.

10. Buelah Brown, "My Winter in Geyserland," *Livingston Enterprise Yellowstone Daily Tourist Edition,* June 20, 1924, sec. 2, p. 4.

Chapter Five
Yellowstone Today

Overindulging at the famous breakfast buffet at the Old Faithful Inn; eating huckleberry ice cream while waiting for Old Faithful geyser; plugging your nose against the smell of rotten eggs when it finally erupts. Many of the memories people take home from Yellowstone today are closely connected to the foods they ate while they were there. The food traditions that began in Yellowstone hundreds of years ago continue throughout the park today. While you are busy hiking, geyser gazing, boating, and wildlife watching, don't forget to stop and engage your senses. Listen to the wind and birds, smell the sulfur, and grab another handful of trail mix. Mmm . . . Yellowstone!

HOTELS TODAY

Restaurants, dining rooms, cafeterias, and grills serve millions of Yellowstone visitors each year. Every eatery offers something unique, and with the variety of food choices around the park, few visitors walk away unsatisfied. Many items on the menus have been served continuously in Yellowstone for decades, while new items appear on the menu every year. Jim Chapman, executive chef at the Yellowstone National Park lodges, shares some of the recipes he uses to tempt travelers'

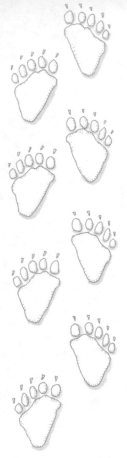

taste buds. Try them at home, but remember that the setting and the atmosphere is often what makes a meal memorable.[1]

Wild Alaska Salmon Poached in Court Bouillon with Cucumbers, Tomato, and Dill

1 ½ pounds wild Alaska salmon fillets

½ gallon court bouillon (recipe follows)

2 cucumbers

2 tomatoes

2 tablespoons chopped shallots

1 cup white wine

2 cups crème fraîche or sour cream

Salt and white pepper to taste

2 tablespoons chopped fresh dill

Portion salmon into four 6-ounce pieces. Heat court bouillon to 180 degrees just below a simmer. Peel cucumbers, split lengthwise, scoop out seeds with a spoon, and slice ¼-inch crescents. Peel, seed, and dice tomatoes. Prepare tomatoes by scooping out core and scoring an X on opposite side, drop tomato into boiling water for 15 seconds, and then shock in cold water. Skin will peel off easily with paring knife. Cut tomato in half crosswise, squeeze and scoop out seeds, dice into 1/4-inch cubes. Place fish in pan with court bouillon; do not stack. Cook until done. Fish will be firm but not mushy in about 12 minutes, depending on the thickness of the fillets. While fish is poaching, make sauce by reducing white wine with shallots by half. Add crème fraîche, bring to simmer, add cucumbers and diced tomatoes and season with salt and pepper. Check taste and consistency, and finish with chopped dill just before serving. Serve with white rice or boiled potatoes.

Court Bouillon

½ gallon water

4 ounces white wine vinegar

4 ounces onion, sliced

2 ounces celery, sliced

2 ounces carrots, sliced

1 ounce salt

¼ teaspoon peppercorns

1 bay leaf

⅛ ounce fresh thyme on branch

5 parsley stems

Combine all ingredients in sauce pot and bring to boil. Reduce heat and simmer for 30 minutes. Strain and cool or keep hot if using right away.

Sweet and Sour Conservation Beef Meatballs

2 slices white bread

1 pound ground conservation beef

1 egg, beaten

¼ cup minced onion

¼ cup beef broth

½ teaspoon minced garlic

½ teaspoon salt

½ teaspoon paprika

¼ teaspoon black pepper

Pinch dried thyme

½ pound plum tomatoes, canned and peeled

¼ cup brown sugar

¼ cup sugar

¼ cup gingersnaps, crumbled

4 tablespoons lemon juice

Preheat oven to 350 degrees.

Soak bread in cold water two minutes, drain, and squeeze out excess water.

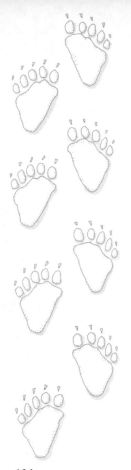

Combine bread with beef, egg, onion, beef broth, garlic, salt, paprika, pepper, and thyme.

Shape into balls and bake until 155 degrees internal temperature.

Drain tomatoes. Heat with sugars, gingersnaps, and lemon juice until the sugar dissolves.

Puree, add meatballs, and simmer until glazed. Sauce can be thickened with a little cornstarch if necessary. Yields 25 meatballs.

Marinated Niman Ranch Pork Chops with Stir-Fried Cabbage

8 5-ounce pork chops	½ teaspoon salt
1 ¼ cup peanut oil	¼ teaspoon pepper
1 teaspoon dry mustard	1 tablespoon caraway seeds
1 teaspoon minced garlic	1 pound shredded cabbage
1 tablespoon chopped fresh rosemary	¼ cup cider vinegar
1 tablespoon minced shallot	Salt and pepper to taste

Marinate pork chops with 1 cup oil, mustard, rosemary, garlic, shallots, salt, and pepper for at least four hours.

Drain marinade and grill pork chops.

While pork chops cook, heat ¼ cup oil in sauté pan and toast caraway seeds until aromatic, add cabbage and toss until heated, add vinegar, and let steam for 30 seconds. Finish with salt and pepper.

Roosevelt Beans

1 pound hamburger or sausage

½ pound bacon, ½-inch dice

1 onion, ½-inch dice

1 can pork and beans, 16 ounces

1 can kidney beans, 12 ounces

1 can lima beans, 12 ounces

1 can butter beans, 12 ounces

½ cup brown sugar

2 tablespoons cider vinegar

1 tablespoon mustard, prepared

½ cup ketchup

Salt and pepper to taste

Fry meats. Drain fat. Sauté onions with meat. Stir in next 10 ingredients. (For a thicker product, drain liquid from beans.) Bake at 325 degrees for 45 minutes.

ROCKY ROADS

Complaining about roads has always been a favorite pastime of Yellowstone tourists. Since the first automobiles entered the park in 1915, the roads have been too windy, too bumpy, too fast, too slow, too hilly, too narrow, and under too much construction. Road crews in Yellowstone fight a never-ending battle against the wintertime frost heaves that rattle the roadbeds. Mudslides can destroy a road in just minutes, and earthquakes, such as the 7.5 quake of 1959, ripple solid asphalt like waves on a waterbed.

As you drive along Yellowstone's rocky roads, consider the fact that you are driving on essentially the same route that tourists traveled 100 years ago. With a few exceptions, the cur-

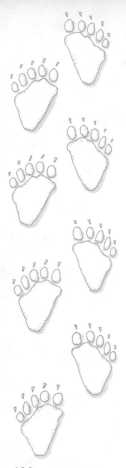

rent figure-eight system follows the path once traveled by stagecoach. Remember that this route was carefully chosen not only to take you to the most popular attractions but also to provide a soothing, leisurely view of the park. So slow down, take a good look, and enjoy your rocky road.

Rocky Road

2 pounds milk or semisweet chocolate

16 ounces miniature marshmallows

2 cups nuts (pecans, walnuts, peanuts, or almonds)

Turn oven on at lowest setting. Cut chocolate into chunks. Place in a heat-resistant container. Turn off oven and put chocolate on the oven rack to melt. Stir occasionally, turning oven on briefly if necessary. Do not overheat.

Remove chocolate from oven and stir until smooth, allowing chocolate to cool slightly but not harden.

Add nuts and stir to coat.

Dab a small amount of chocolate on a clean fingertip to check temperature. When chocolate is cool enough not to melt them, add marshmallows. Stir until well covered with chocolate.

Spread a sheet of waxed paper over a cookie sheet. Pour chocolate mixture onto cookie sheet. Use a rubber spatula to scrape sides of the bowl—but not too well, so there's something left to lick clean! Spread the chocolate mixture over the cookie sheet with spatula, forming a lumpy layer from ½ to 1 inch thick.

Chill until chocolate hardens. (The impatient cook can stick the cookie sheet in the freezer for about an hour. Otherwise, chill in refrigerator at least 4 hours.)

After candy sets, break into bite-size pieces. Serve in a candy dish or individual paper cups.

HOWARD EATON TRAIL MIX

Getting away from the roads and crowds on a day hike is a popular way to explore Yellowstone. Even with 306 miles of road in Yellowstone, you can only see 2 percent of the park from the window of your car. Hundreds of waterfalls, meadows, geysers, and lakes lie beyond the roads, waiting for you to explore them.

One individual mourned the popularity of stagecoach/automobile travel in Yellowstone, longing for the day when travelers could explore the park without seeing another soul. Howard Eaton established a trail system that connected popular areas of the park on a 150-mile route following roughly the same course as the roads, but putting enough distance between trail and road that users of the trail system could experience Yellowstone without vehicles.

Though Eaton led horseback trips over that route for many years, the wilderness has reclaimed much of the original trail. The parts that survived have been incorporated into today's trail system as the Howard Eaton Trail. Pieces of it pop up all over the park, from Mammoth to Lake. So next time you want to get off the road and onto a beaten path, grab some trail mix for a hike to Cascade Lake along the old Howard Eaton Trail.

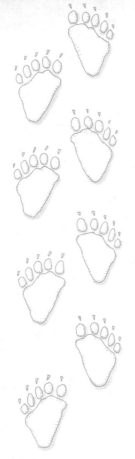

Howard Eaton Trail Mix

6 cups dry cereal (puffed corn Kix)

2 cups nuts (cashews, almonds, and/or peanuts)

½ cup raisins

1 cup banana chips

1 cup candy-coated chocolate pieces

1 3-ounce package butterscotch pudding (not instant)

½ cup honey

⅔ cup peanut butter

Stir together cereal, nuts, raising, banana chips, and chocolate pieces in a large mixing bowl.

Mix pudding and honey in a small saucepan. Heat over medium high until mixture starts to boil. Boil 30 seconds and remove from heat.

Stir in peanut butter and mix until smooth.

Pour over cereal mixture while stirring. Toss until well coated.

Spread mixture onto a cookie sheet to cool. When hardened, break up large chunks and store in large resealable bags for the trail.

MUNCHING ON THE TRAIL

Apples or Oranges? Fruits are excellent for hiking because they provide simple sugars for a natural energy boost. When choosing a fruit to stash in your pack, remember that you can't leave even a core or peel behind. Remember to bring along a plastic bag to pack out the peel, or consider peeling your orange before you go.

Cascade Lake can be reached from two trailheads: one just west of Canyon Junction and one north of the junction at the Cascade Lake picnic area. Both trails are relatively flat, following the edges of meadow and forest to the lake itself, a distance of 2.5 miles. These meadows are well-grazed by wildlife, particularly bison and occasionally moose. Wear your boots, for the trail near the lake stays muddy through most of the summer. From Cascade Lake the Howard Eaton Trail continues on to Grebe, Wolf, and Ice lakes, ending on the opposite side of the upper loop near the Norris Campground. Conditions on this trail vary, so check in at a visitor center before attempting the entire fifteen-mile hike.

Protein power: Throw in some high-protein munchies to keep you satisfied and energized all day long. Trail mixes and mixed nuts provide sustaining energy on your day hike. While sugar gives you a quick energy burst, protein builds up a reserve of energy and releases it slowly, allowing you to keep hiking mile after mile. Remember to bring extra water if you'll be munching on salty snacks.

Lunch on the go: No matter how carefully you pack your bag, it seems your lunch will always end up on the bottom. Packing your food in lightweight plastic containers is a great way to keep that sandwich from turning into a pancake along the way.

"Water, water everywhere, nor any drop to drink": Many of Yellowstone's streams look crystal clear and wonderfully cool, but don't be fooled. Microorganisms live in almost all Yellowstone

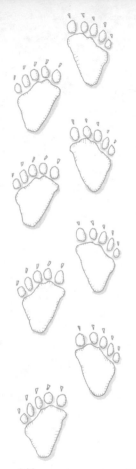

water, hot or cold. Many of these are harmless, but some of them can cause serious illness. The stream-loving parasite *Giardia lamblia* can cause serious intestinal distress, while some of the hot-water organisms can cause meningitis (an inflammation of the brain and spinal cord) or Legionnaires' disease (a respiratory disease caused by the bacteria *Legionella pneumophila*). Geologists have also found traces of arsenic and mercury in Yellowstone's thermal pools, so a sip from a hot spring could be fatal. To protect the pools and the visitors, laws prohibit drinking from thermal features.

It's always a good idea to pack enough water for your hike (at least one quart; more for longer hikes) and purify any water before refilling your bottles. While many people use pumps or chemical treatments, boiling is the simplest and most effective way to treat water in the backcountry. Boil water at night for drinking the next day, letting it stand and cool overnight.

Banana Boats on Yellowstone Lake

Yellowstone Lake is not the largest lake in the country, nor is it the coldest, deepest, or most remote. It is, however, a lake unlike any other. Framed by the Absaroka Mountains, with peaks towering over 11,000 feet in elevation, Yellowstone Lake is one of the most scenic areas of the park. It is also one of the most geologically interesting places in the world.

Half of the lake sits within the Yellowstone caldera, and its shape is largely due to volcanic activity in the area. About 150,000 years ago, a volcanic explosion, roughly the same size as the Mount Saint Helens eruption in 1980, blew out a massive crater near the lake. That crater was

RECOMMENDED DAY HIKES IN YELLOWSTONE

Fairy Falls/Imperial Geyser (6.4 miles): *This flat, easy trail winds through marshy meadows and forests burned in the 1988 fires to Fairy Falls, a 197-foot waterfall nestled in a shady cove along the rocky cliff. After cooling by the falls, take the 0.7-mile spur trail to Imperial Geyser. Keeping a careful distance from the thermal features, peer into the massive crater of Imperial Geyser, and watch, if you're lucky, its fifty-foot eruptions.*

Mount Washburn (6 miles): *Two trails access the summit of this 10,243-foot peak, both of similar length and difficulty. The Chittenden Road access traverses steep meadows with views of the mountain ranges to the north and west. The Dunraven Pass trail begins south of the peak and ascends through forested areas, then offers stunning views of Yellowstone Lake and the caldera as it approaches the summit. Whatever side you choose, you will be hiking along a historic road. Early Yellowstone travelers could drive to the top of Mount Washburn on the road you are now hiking. Before you get too envious of their easy ride to the top, adjust your mental image to show the train of Model Ts driving up the trail you are on . . . backward. Early automobiles were not equipped with fuel pumps, so in order to keep fuel in the engine on the steep incline, the hood had to remain lower than the rear. Everybody look out—Dad is driving up the mountain in reverse!*

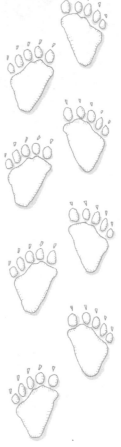

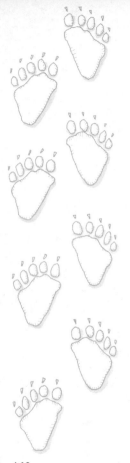

Delacey Creek (6 miles): *Wander with Delacey Creek through tall forest and vast meadows as it winds its way to Shoshone Lake. This deep, 8,000-acre lake is considered the largest lake in the lower forty-eight states that is not accessible by road. When you reach the gravelly lakeshore (made of glassy volcanic rocks like obsidian), poke a finger or two in the lake. Chilly? Shoshone Lake rarely gets warmer than 62 degrees Fahrenheit. If you were submerged in water that cold, it would take only minutes for hypothermia to set in. Brr!*

Trout Lake (1.2 miles): *This popular fishing lake is also a haven for a variety of wildlife. A short, half-mile trail ascends steeply through a Douglas fir forest to Trout Lake, where an unofficial path circles the twelve-acre lake. In late June the inlet on the north side of the lake becomes a major aquatic traffic jam. Spawning trout choke the creek as they scramble upstream to lay and fertilize eggs. If you miss the spawning season, turn your attention to the trees where you may see eagles or osprey scanning the lake for signs of dinner. On a summer evening you may also see otters splashing on the lake shores.*

South Rim/Clear Lake (4.5 miles): *Park roads offer several stunning views of the Grand Canyon of the Yellowstone, but the canyon's sheer cliffs, pastel colors, and immense size are better absorbed by walking along the rim. For this four-and-a-half-mile loop, leave your vehicle at the Uncle Tom's trailhead on the road to Artist Point. Take the trail to Clear Lake, crossing the south rim road and heading through a broad meadow south of the park-*

ing area (watch for bison!) The trail winds through several backcountry thermal areas, which you will likely smell long before you see them. Approach all thermal features with caution, remembering that solid-looking ground can be quite unstable. *Turn left at the first junction toward Clear Lake, then left again to Lily Lake, both of which are aptly named: a translucent pond and an oblong lake covered with hundreds of pond lilies. After circling Lily Lake, you come abruptly to the brink of the canyon. The next section of trail is not for those fearful of heights: below you the canyon walls slide 1,200 feet to the Yellowstone River. The last mile and a half follow the rim of the canyon, rising and falling over several hills and periodically touching the brink of the canyon for magnificent views of Upper and Lower Falls (109 and 306 feet tall, respectively). If you still have the energy, at Uncle Tom's Trail you can descend 328 steps for a spectacular close-up of the Lower Falls—just remember that you have to come back up again.*

Storm Point (2.5 miles): *With its 110 miles of shoreline, Lake Yellowstone can't be circled on a day hike, but the hike to Storm Point offers a dazzling taste of the lake's splendor. This loop trail hits the lakeshore on a rocky point named for the ferocious storms that hit land on this northern part of the lake. On a still day you can enjoy the reflection of the Absaroka Mountains in the tranquil waters, before circling back to the trailhead.*

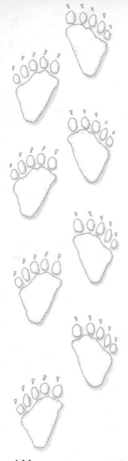

filled with water, giving the lake its western extension called West Thumb. Other explosions have changed the shape of the lake as well, such as the hydrothermal explosion at Mary Bay. This bay was formed when hot water and steam built up enough pressure underground to burst through the surface, throwing rocks five miles in every direction.

The Yellowstone hotspot continues to alter the shape of the lake. As the magma chamber huffs and puffs below the surface, it moves the ground above it up and down. As the caldera rises, the northern part of the lake, which rests over the hotspot, pushes up. This uplift has tipped the lake to the south, flooding some of the trees along the southern shores, causing false concern that the lake level was rising.

During the summer of 2003, Yellowstone Lake was again a site of alarm, capturing a national and international media spotlight. Researchers with the U.S. Geologic Survey have been mapping a previously undetected bulge in the bottom of the lake. Reports of the "inflated plane" brought panic: Is this a sign that the Yellowstone volcano is ready to blow? Global headlines predicted the worst. As rumors flew, researchers had a hard time explaining what they were *really* looking at on the lake floor. Yes, there was an uplift. Yes, there is thermal activity on the bottom of the lake. But the bulge was not necessarily new to the lake. It may have sat there for thousands of years, unnoticed, until the research equipment improved enough to "see" it below the water.

After a day spent boating on the Yellowstone Lake or hiking along its shore, throw some Banana Boats on the campfire for a warm dessert to end a cool day.

Banana Boats on Yellowstone Lake

Bananas

Miniature marshmallows

Chocolate chips

Brown sugar

Slit each banana lengthwise, but do not peel. Hollow out a wedge-shaped section from the fruit (which you can eat!) Fill the hollow with as many marshmallows and chocolate chips as will fit, probably not much more than one or two teaspoons each. Sprinkle mixture with brown sugar. Close banana and wrap tightly with aluminum foil. Heat in campfire coals for five to seven minutes, allowing chocolate and marshmallows to melt. Eat while warm, scraping out the banana peel boat with an oar-shaped spoon.

LAKE OVERLOOK TRAIL

An easy, two-mile loop trail leaving from the West Thumb geyser basin offers incredible views of Yellowstone Lake and the mountains rising above it in the east. The Lake Overlook Trail begins in the geyser basin parking lot and winds through burned lodgepole forest as it climbs 200 feet for a breathtaking view (taking all the breath you have left after that short but steep climb).

Snowballs in July

Many park rangers roll their eyes when they are issued an "up-to-date" weather forecast for Yellowstone National Park. Trying to predict the weather in Yellowstone is like trying to predict where to find a bear: you might get in the general area, but by then the bear has probably moved on. Dramatic variation in elevation and topography creates weather fluctuations that can drive a meteorologist wild (not to mention the crowds of tourists who just laid out a picnic lunch). Thus it is not unusual to get trapped behind a snowplow clearing seven inches of snow off the ground in the middle of July. Nor is it unusual start off the day in Mammoth Hot Springs wearing shorts and a T-shirt, put on a sweatshirt while walking the rim of the canyon, and wrap up the day at Lake Village in a hat, scarf, gloves, and raincoat. Sunny days at Old Faithful are often stormy days at other places in the park, and vice versa.

So be prepared for all types of weather on your visit to Yellowstone. But try not to worry too much—if you don't like the weather, just give it a few minutes and it will likely change. And if you find yourself waiting out a hot day, wishing for that July snowstorm, pull out some of these snowball treats which will last, even on the hottest of days.

Snowballs in July

¾ cup peanut butter
¾ cup honey

½ cup semisweet chocolate chips
½ cup chopped pecans

½ cup granola

½ cup crisp rice cereal

¾ cup graham cracker crumbs

1 cup shredded coconut

Combine peanut butter and honey in a large microwave safe bowl. Microwave 30 seconds and blend until smooth. If still lumpy, microwave another 30 seconds. Cool.

Add the rest of the ingredients, except coconut, and mix until coated.

Generously butter hands and scoop tablespoonfuls of mixture from the bowl. Roll between palms to form a ball, then drop onto a plate of coconut. Roll each ball in coconut until well coated, then transfer to a cookie sheet lined with waxed paper. Chill in refrigerator.

Hot "Chocolate Pots" Cocoa

There's nothing quite like winding down with a cup of hot cocoa after a long day of exploring Yellowstone. The only thing Willy Wonka has on Yellowstone is fountains that gush with pure milk chocolate. One feature in Yellowstone manages to come close to a fountain of chocolate, so much so that its discoverers called it the Chocolate Pots. This spring runs with clear, hot water and look like any other hot spring on the surface. But if you were to dip a cupful of the water out of the springs, you could watch it turn to chocolate before your eyes! Okay, so it's not really chocolate, but iron. As the water cools, it releases the iron it has been able to absorb underground through heat and pressure. Those iron molecules band together and turn the water as brown as chocolate.

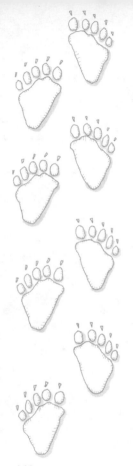

Chocolate Pots Cocoa

Cocoa mix:

2 ½ cups powdered sugar	1 ½ cups cocoa
¾ cup brown sugar	1 teaspoon salt
1 cup granulated sugar	10 cups powdered milk

Mix dry ingredients together and store in a large can. Makes about 1 gallon of mix. Can also be stored in smaller containers for easy packing on your trip to Yellowstone.

To serve:

Heat water on the stove or campfire (be careful to put a lid on so your water doesn't fill with ash from the fire). Pour hot water into mugs. Pour 3 heaping spoonfuls cocoa mix into hot water and stir until dissolved. Add more cocoa if desired. Top with marshmallows, a peppermint stick, a dollop of whipped cream, or a splash of cold milk. Sit back, take a sip, and relax around the fire.

SOME MORE S'MORES

Generations of campers have been munching on s'mores, the traditional campfire dessert with the funny name. Most of us remember toasting (and often torching) marshmallows over the fire, then squishing them between graham cracker squares and chunks of cold chocolate bar. S'mores have traditionally combined these three ingredients, but if you ask around, you may find that someone else's s'more looks nothing like your own. Next time you are lingering around a campfire, try one of these variations on an old favorite.

Sweet and Salty S'mores

Round, butter-flavored crackers   Chocolate bar
Peanut butter   Marshmallows

Spread peanut butter on the side of one cracker; place your chocolate square on the other. Toast your marshmallow and sandwich in between.

Black and White S'mores

Chocolate-flavored graham crackers   Marshmallows
Cream cheese

Spread a thin layer of cream cheese (use flavored if you like) on both sides of the graham cracker. Toast marshmallow and sandwich.

Peanut Butter and Jelly S'mores

Graham crackers   Jam or jelly
Peanut butter   Marshmallows

Coat one graham cracker with peanut butter and drizzle the other one with jam. Toast marshmallows and press between the crackers.

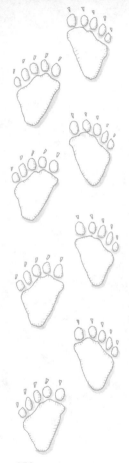

As you sit around the fire, sipping a cup of cocoa and roasting the ever handy marshmallows, enjoy a scrumptious story from Yellowstone's past. Then see if you can concoct some legends of your own—and don't be afraid to spice it up, mountain-man style, with a little flavorful embellishment. After all, in Yellowstone, anything's possible.

Notes

1. Recipes courtesy Xanterra Parks and Resorts in Yellowstone National Park and Jim Chapman, executive chef.

⇢ Index of Recipes ⇠

→About the Author←

After a long day answering questions at the Mammoth Hot Springs visitor center, Melanie Armstrong was winding down, eating a bowl of chocolate chip ice cream, when another ranger shared a trick for identifying animal droppings. "You can always recognize deer scat," she said, "because it looks like chocolate chips." Melanie never finished that bowl of ice cream, but from that day on she could easily identify deer scat when she saw it along Yellowstone's trails. She began collecting food-related stories from other rangers, as well as culinary histories from the park archives, and used them in her programs to show visitors that the strange things going on in Yellowstone were not so different from the things happening back home in their kitchens.

When she's not leading tours through Norris Geyser Basin or hiking in the backcountry, Melanie relaxes in the kitchen. Living an hour from the nearest grocery store often demands creative cooking, particularly when you come home from work to find just a can of beans and a jar of peanut butter in the cupboard. She thanks the hearty rangers who sampled her cooking experiments while swapping stories around the campfire. This book is dedicated to them and to the park they love.

During the winter, Melanie migrates south to Albuquerque, New Mexico, where she is working toward a degree in American Studies. She still enjoys ice cream—but hold the chocolate chips.